THE
WAY
IT
works
WITH
women

THE WAY IT works WITH *women*

LOUIS CALAFERTE

Translated from the French by Sarah Harrison

THE MARLBORO PRESS/NORTHWESTERN
NORTHWESTERN UNIVERSITY PRESS
EVANSTON, ILLINOIS

The Marlboro Press/Northwestern
Northwestern University Press
www.nupress.northwestern.edu

Originally published in French in 1992 under the title *La mécanique des femmes*. Copyright © 1992 by Éditions Gallimard. English translation copyright © 1998 by Sarah Harrison. Published 1998. All rights reserved.

Printed in the United States of America

ISBN 978-0-8101-6094-1

The Library of Congress has cataloged the original, hardcover edition as follows:

Calaferte, Louis, 1928–
    [Mécanique des femmes. English]
    The way it works with women / Louis Calaferte ; translated from the French by Sarah Harrison.
      p. cm.
    ISBN 0-8101-6033-1 (cloth)
    1. Women—Sexual behavior—Fiction. I. Harrison, Sarah. II. Title.
    PQ2663.A389M4313 1998
    848'.913—dc21   98-23814
                                     CIP

Ce n'est pas la femme, c'est le sexe. Ce n'est pas le sexe, c'est l'instant—la folie de le diviser, l'instant—ou celle d'atteindre... quoi?

Ce n'est pas le plaisir—c'est le mouvement qu'il imprime, c'est le changement qu'il demande, harcèle, et devant lequel il retombe, brisé, rompu, couronné d'une jouissance, liquéfié, achevé, béat, mais la volupté cache sa défaite.

— **PAUL VALÉRY,**
Cahiers, II, Éros

EARLY MORNING IN HOTEL ROOMS WHERE ONE HAS done no sleeping, strangely empty, silent. One wishes the world might stand still while, in the bed, spent from the night, the little body curled up under the covers rests, half sunk in a somnolence which will soon interrupt itself for the separation the new day will bring.

—You never think about death?

She whirls round gaily.

—I'm young!

—I'm being serious with you. Don't you ever think about death?

Pressing down into her skirt, she places her hand in the hollow where her thighs come together.

—I think about this. It's the same thing.

With an expression of contempt.

—You want to make me die a little?

Arching her back, she thrusts her sex forward.

—And with this you can die over and over. Want to try? I'm a nice little death-dealing whore.

—I'm asking you if you never think of death?

Furious, stony eyed.

—Screw you and your death! Me, I fuck, and while I'm fucking I fucking don't give a damn about death!

Throwing herself angrily into an armchair.

—Go on, jerk off on death.

Drawing close to her.

—Don't touch me.

She buries her face in her folded arms.

—I don't want anyone talking to me about death.

Her voice now shrill.

—Me, I'm alive, I'm alive!

I light a cigarette.

—What are you so afraid of?

Shooting up as though electrified.

—The devil, if you want to know! Satan! Lucifer! The devil!

She laughs crazily through her tears.

A mauve ribbon.

—Give me your hand, I'll take you through the streets you love.

Surrounded by the people in there, her eyes never leave me, fastened on mine, little burning black pebbles, her face expressionless, she removes the ice cube from her glass and licks it with an enveloping tongue, twisting it nonchalantly before her parted lips, the next instant slipping it down into the bodice of her summer dress, brings it out again, holds it up in her palm till the warmth there melts it into little droplets which she catches with the tip of her tongue before tucking it into her mouth where she shifts it from cheek to cheek before finally spitting it out into her glass enveloped in a long driblet of foamy saliva, then letting her eyelids sink heavily as though smitten by love's blessed weariness.

Narrow and dark, the wooden stairway at the hotel.
—Can you see my panties as I go up?
—Just a peep.
—You have a hard on?
—Naturally.
—What color are they?
—Blue.

She throws herself into my arms. Supple body.
—I just got myself shafted out there, in the street. I still have his dried come on my thighs.
Her breath in my ear.
—Talk to me.
Her hard thighs locked round my hips.
—Tell me I'm a whore.
A short grating laugh.
—You don't dare say it, do you? Huh?
Her warm tongue's wetness.
—Whore.

—Pretty little whore.

—Pretty little whore.

—Sweet little whore.

—Sweet little whore.

Her head with its tousled hair beating against my chest.

—With you I get hot.

Teeth nipping at my skin, biting.

—I never forget a man who could get me hot.

Dumpy, wrinkled, watery eyed, planted there amidst the passersby, her worn handbag clutched to her belly.

She steps forward hesitantly.

—Want to see me with nothing on?

On the sidewalk the crowd presses in both directions.

—I have the best tits in the world.

She is old, pitiful.

Her hand in mine, pulling me to a building in the poor area where a long narrow entranceway leads to a cramped courtyard lit by a grizzling sky threatening rain.

—Look.

She lifts some woolen swaddlings, darned and faded.

—See how beautiful they are?

Empty bags, flat, drooping flaps of flabby white.

—You can touch.

—I have five cocks all for myself. At the moment the one I am fondest of is my chilly little prick.

Raising her hollowed palm to her face to sniff it.
—Anyone ever tell you your jizz smells good?
She runs the tip of her tongue rapidly over her fingers.

In the dark she bolts into the public square, runs up to
a tree and throws her arms around it, and, as in lovemaking, humps her body against it, then rubs it with her sex,
her hands clutching her breasts, her head thrown back, her
mouth open, letting out little gasps of pleasure.

On the open bed, its sheets thrown back, she, naked
and grave with the gravity of her youth, uncertain at this
moment she has wished for, now lifts her hand imperceptibly.
—Come here, I want to make you die.

—Let me into your pocket, I'll get it up for you while
we walk.

Her traveling bag is filled with clothes.
—I am going to change all night long, I am going to
transform myself, metamorphose for you. I'll be an innocent little girl, a young woman, a woman of the world, a
housekeeper, a whore. How do you prefer me? I'll begin
with the primmest and go right through to the total slut.
By the time I've done them all, your cock'll be sick for me.

The red imprint of her lips on a letter.

The train pulls away. From behind a window, the young blond girl stares out at me, flicking the tip of her tongue.

—I want to spit on you.

—I am spitting on you.

—I am spitting on your cock.

—I'm full of juice and I'm spitting my juice all over you.

—Does my saliva smell?

—My saliva smells of the devil.

—I spit devil when I spit.

—There's a pin at the neck of my dress because one of the buttons has fallen off.

—Can you see my thighs through the opening of my dress?

—Get down on the floor.

—I want to walk on you.

—I have you underfoot.

—I want to crush your balls with my heels.

—Can you see my panties? What's it like?

—Can you see any hairs?

—It's my pussy that's eating up your balls.

—I would like to get into all your holes.

—I am about to spit into your mouth.

—Spit into my mouth again.

—I want you to spit on me.

—Go on, spit on me.

Long skinny legs, straight, too white under the cupola of her stale worn dress.

She has a harsh voice, untidy red hair, big hands with spiderlike fingers, there's always a little spittle at the corners of her mouth, she doesn't smell nice, instead of walking it's like she hops around on her long legs, the way insects do, in summertime.

Every time she wants us to go over by the abandoned cement works, where there are puddles of red mud, rats that run away squealing, and scary big black birds.

If you refuse to follow her she flies into a rage.

—You'll see, you little piece of shit! The dogs'll eat it right off you! You'll bleed all over the place and you'll have no itsy-bitsy left, it'll serve you right, should've come with me to the cement works, you've come before, you already know what I do, don't you? Doesn't hurt, does it? I don't bite, not me. You'll be sorry when the dogs from up there come and eat it right off, but it'll be too late. Anyway, at the cement works I've got all the cocks I want, yours isn't the only one. Go ahead, give yours to the dogs up there, that's all it's good for! I don't like yours, to start with. It stinks. It's too small. It'll really crack me up the day the dogs eat it off you. Above all, don't ever come begging me anymore to eat it for you. I've got others, fortunately, bigger ones! I'll tell the dogs that and they'll come eat it off! They know me, they do what I say. You'll have no cock left, they'll eat your nuts along with it, you'll have nothing left, like a girl! . . . Oh! The girlie! The girlie! . . .

Soft roundness of her breasts beneath the pink wool of her jacket.

—Have you noticed?

She is sitting on a bench in the restaurant, I on a somewhat higher chair facing and looking down at her.

—I've no brassiere, does it show?

She glances down at her chest.

—They're not very big but it shows all the same, I'd say.

Her leg inserts itself between mine under the table.

—I've no panties on either. I'm ready to be fucked anywhere.

Her full plate in front of her.

—Let's eat, then you fuck me, right away in the first doorway we find. The skirt I have on unbuttons.

She has her hair done, is wearing light makeup, has on trousers and a tightly nipped-in waistcoat, a laceration, that is what such beauty makes her into.

She holds my hand as we walk.

—What I love is when I've done one and have the feeling my pussy's still open.

At night, she is unable to go home, everything about the streets draws her, the solitary walkers, the drunks, the crazies, the prostitutes, the police roundups, the ghostly figures you catch glimpses of, the petrified life of the cafés, the lights, the couples leaning against walls clutched in each other's embrace, the woman gabbling incoherently, the cars slowing down alongside her, the driver who cranks down his window and whistles to her, she goes over to him or doesn't, if she declines, they insult her, which she doesn't really mind, the poorer neighborhoods, almost deserted, the elevated train gliding like a long toy in the night, the men who follow her from street to street without coming up to her and whose steps are suddenly no longer heard, the fatigue mounting within her like a cold tide, she would like to be in her bed after taking a shower but, at the same time, still be here, the youth who has been knocked off his motorbike by the car belonging to a young couple, who stand dumbly on the curb before his body with its bloody head and hands, the someone who approaches, who intentionally brushes against her, she calls him a dirty name and he goes away, limping, why not go to bed with a cripple? police sirens at her back, the air has cooled, she shivers, the young man's blood was black on the ground, will she die one night in the street? she does not want to think of death, it's late, she'll not go home yet, she knows a café where she can pick up a man, she would like to take a taxi, once she sucked off the driver and the ride had been free, how many men had she sucked off? why do men so love to be sucked off? there's a crowd gathering at the end of the avenue, she crosses over, someone is following her, she'll look back pretty soon, if he's young she'll fuck him, she has a strong wish to make love, to have an orgasm, most of them unload and leave, but a deep orgasm and then to sleep until tomorrow, must find a decent hotel, they all choose cheap hotels, there are also those who want to do it fast in the first alley they can find, tonight she would like, she doesn't know what she would like, if it were a very grand hotel, a really beautiful room, she turns round, all stooped over, old guy, the poor asshole, who do they think they are all these creeps? if she needs a cock there're plenty to choose from, dawn is nearly here, she stops a taxi and has him take her to an address, the most exciting thing is knowing, as she climbs the stairs or takes the elevator, that the cock up there waiting for her is already hard, sometimes, in order to really enjoy that erection behind the door, she doesn't ring the bell right away, the night is a flaming madness.

—You know who I am?
Ironic.
—An utter debauchee.
Her lascivious movement.
—Debauched, lewd, corrupt, out of control; voluptuous, immoral, licentious, dissolute, sensual, smutty, a full-time fucker, depraved, indecent, game for anything.
Kissing my hand with feigned devotion.
—And despite all that I want to be loved.

In the vacant courtyard, a chained dog's plaintive barking.

She writes:
Since I have come to know you, I like to walk around naked in my kitchen. I like knowing that you would love to see me thus.

A so to speak biological incapacity to register and report anything whatever that she has seen or experienced in the preceeding instant. Questioning her, you only get an exasperating silence which finally inspires compassion for this little girl that the world in movement seems to pass by.

I smile at her. She looks at me, first with a bit of fearfulness, then in turn tries a timid smile, stares at her shoes, her hands folded one on top of the other upon her stomach.

What I do then is whistle, and instantly she is skipping about the room as though she has forgotten everything that has just taken place.

—You know, I like you all right. Yes, I do like you, all right.

She halts in front of the window, her forehead touching the pane. On my side, I pretend to be busy.

With solemn conviction:

—Yes, you, I like you all right.

The wooden shutters are closed against the heat, from which the rafters, the flashing, and the roof tiles are sizzling. Chinks between the laths let in knife blades of metallic white light in which dust motes dance. From outside comes the unbearable rasping of some insect.

On the bed, half-naked, she stares ahead of her at the portrait of a woman hanging on the wall, a beautiful sad face, the neck adorned with a string of big black pearls, a tortoiseshell fan held shut in her hand.

—Every time I look at her I ask myself how she used to make love.

Thoughtfully.

—Do you think she had a lot of men?

A quick, almost imperceptible smile.

—As many as me?

Silence.

—I don't know why I'm such a slut. I think I've always been this way.

The curve of her shoulder.

—It's all I ever wanted.

Lifting her eyes.

—How about it, do I seem like a terrific whore to you?

They live together, but it's exactly like they were strangers, it's difficult to talk about, especially to a man, and yet it's the truth, she isn't exaggerating, it's been over three years since he's got near her, it's not him, it's her, she doesn't want to anymore, not since she found out he'd slept with a man, a friend of theirs, who however wasn't a homosexual, in appearance anyway, but it had nevertheless happened all right, and as soon as she found out about it, it was finished between them, she finds him repulsive, were she to consent she'd have the impression he was fucking this guy and not her, she doesn't know exactly how they go about it, men, but she's sure it's something absolutely disgusting, all those hairs together, she would rather not think about it, it sickens her, fortunately the children don't know, don't suspect anything, for the boys it would be terrible, maybe worse even than for her, do they do everything like with a woman? if you picture some things it's enough to put you off making love for the rest of your life, he'd come back with his thing just out of the other and stick it into her? she'd rather die, naturally she'd thought about leaving him, but there are the children, they love their father, respect him, they have no idea what he has turned into, if they found out the oldest would kill him, sometimes, at the table, the boys make jokes on the subject, she doesn't dare look at her husband, she goes into the kitchen and stays there a long while before coming back, to do this to a woman, there is nothing worse, had he cheated on her normally she would have understood, it wouldn't have been the same shock, from here on, no matter what happens, he isn't going to touch her, she'd thought of taking a lover, but she can't do it, she imagines they have all slept with other men, young though she is, she can never again have any true sex life.

—I love the light caress of cool fresh cloth on my skin

In a corner, the little blue swallow repeated on the wallpaper.

—You've slept with a lot of men?

—Many.

Her drifting gaze.

—The first time I jerked a man off I was twelve years old.

Then passionately.

—I've often done it, often. I love men.

You weren't supposed to go near where the lady with the beautiful long dresses lived. No one ever spoke to her, not even to say good morning. She kidnapped little boys. Her house was full of them. Loads of little boys that no one had ever seen again, that no one will ever see again because she eats them one after another.

The lady with the beautiful long dresses was a prostitute.

—Stay where you are, don't move.

She goes to the far end of the room where she takes up a pose, one foot on a chair, her thigh bare.

—Have you seen my shoes?

Red shoes, with high heels and laces, that hug the ankle.

—What I like about them are the laces, very whore-like, don't you agree?

Lifting her skirt up against her belly.

—But you haven't yet seen my panties.

Small and black.

—Hardly cover me at all. You can get at me very easily, anywhere.

Her head bent forward within the cascade of her heavy hair. She is sucking hard on one of the loosened laces.

—Do you like that?

Her face turned toward me so that I not miss anything of that image, at the same time childlike yet provocative.

—Stroke yourself while I suck this.

Her tongue, her lips move forward, seeking the shoelace stretched tight between her fingers.

She picks up a handful of snow on the hotel room balcony and, laughing, brings it back to the bed and rubs my cock with it.

—I feel beautiful enough to make the earth tremble.

A body that is but one long satiny shudder.

While seated in the train she wriggles out of fine lace

panties on which there are stains. Slipping them into her pocket, she looks at me, then lowers her eyes, laughs.

With her hair up, her forehead revealed, tall, simple, wearing a pair of tight-fitting trousers, she appears clad in the divineness of beauty, but, as if inside an envelope, the falsely appeased Black Fire is smoldering, ready to burst into flame at the first occasion.

She writes:

All I would like is for you to be a surgeon to me. Cut me up with a little scalpel and eat me.

I am thinking about the tip of your cock, I don't know why it's always the tip that comes back to my mind.

Follow me.

Follow me.

I'll take you window-shopping. I'll have you walking, walking behind me with the delicious sensation of knowing that you can see my legs, my behind, my neck, my hair which stirs, and that you are thinking of what my cunt looks like as I am walking. I would like to feel you behind me, as though we were walking with your cock in my pussy. I'd like to run. My pussy running.

Bite me. I set your teeth on edge.

She gets out of the bed, holding her brassiere between her fingertips, a body with very white skin, a body of massive beauty.

—Don't look at me like that, we don't know each other, I'm a little ashamed, I'm not a whore, I don't usually go with men, you, I fancied you, don't watch me while I'm washing, promise? if you like, I'll come back, I haven't even sucked you off, especially now you must have my taste on you, I live with a friend but so far as fucking goes it's less than nothing, it doesn't keep me from loving him though, it's not something you can explain, maybe it will develop in time, what do you think? I could make love all day long, shut your eyes, I'm sitting down on the bidet, do you think I pass as a fucker? I think so, that's why I'd like my friend to wake up, you may not believe me but I've never yet dared to suck him off, I get the impression he might not like that, so from time to time I spend an hour with someone else, I admit that I do, because finally I miss it, don't look, you're cheating, you promised, when I'm finished I'll come back and suck you off.

It had rained the night before the burial of someone in her family, the cemetery pathways were soaked with water, the women's heels sank into the gravel, next to the grave the pile of earth was yellow and red, greasy like clay.

The casket lowered, the prayers said, while each tossed in a farewell rose she had been unable to keep from taking a handful of that earth, from kneading it a little and then from dropping it down upon the lid in front of her.

—As if all that earth were fuck, a hillock of fuck, I couldn't get the idea out of my head, I had to touch it. Afterward I licked my glove. It was grainy. Some fuck is like that.

The child is standing there eating a cream puff, she is staring in front of her fixedly, tears are running down her cheeks.

Inside the undulating fullness of the long skirt that covers her legs, she advances on all fours, her tongue hanging out.
—I'm hungry. I want some. I'm a little dog.
She barks.

A tube of lipstick.

Sniffing the sweat of the man one loves.

Bouncing up and down on her knees in a big armchair which almost engulfs her small body.
—There's nothing better than a cock.
She sucks her thumb.

The look in those green eyes is outrageous.

She writes:
It's our first night together. It's beautiful and uncertain. Let's tame each other. Let's tell our stories, your mouth against my ear.

—I called to her: "Mummy! I'm bleeding! Mummy! Come and see! I'm bleeding!"

She was at a neighbor's. I was holding my dress up with both hands so as not to stain it. Instead of doing something, reassuring me, talking to me, they laughed like two idiots. Pointing at me my mother said: "That does it, there's another one who'll have herself pregnant before you know it!" I prayed all night.

A light gray check suit over black stockings descending into fancy bright yellow leather shoes.

With her slenderness, her youth, she is beauty's own exasperating elusiveness.

—Can you guess what color my panties are?

Once out of the taxi that had brought us from the station, she casts quick glances at each doorway as we proceed down the street, looking for a place where we could be out of sight and she could show me these famous panties which for her seem to be a symbolic erotic sign.

—I want to show them to you.

Indifferent to the stares of the public then in the midst of dining, she walks through the big restaurant like a conqueror.

A few steps behind her, I see with amazement that she is heading for the toilets where she enters the women's compartment and shutting the door behind us, at once presses back against the wall, with one hand ceremoniously lifting the middle panel of her tight skirt, her eyes riveted on mine, her lips slightly parted.

At last I discover those panties, of a deep red silk,

whose brilliance and apparent softness are in exacerbating harmony with the black net of her stockings.

—They're awfully exciting, don't you think?

From her big handbag she draws a rosebud, which is for me, but before offering it to me she slides it up and down over that, as though fire-enveloped, sex.

—Now smell it.

Her perfume.

—I sprayed it on my panties this morning before leaving home to come and get you.

—You'll be my all-purpose handyman, you'll serve me here in the house, in the afternoon you will accompany me on my errands, in the evening we'll go out together, life will be splendid, I can keep you, but on one condition, that you give it to me every time I want it.

I stub my cigarette out in the big ashtray and head for the door.

That grating voice:

—Go on, go and fuck your little sluts! I'm sure there's not one of them knows how to make love the way I do. And yet you know, don't you, what I can do with a cock? Think you'll find that elsewhere?

She throws herself in front of me.

—What've they got between their legs that makes you chase after them? You're saying I'm not complicated enough for you? Have I told you I've fucked in every country on earth, with men from all over the world, that at twelve I was no longer a virgin?

Detaining me with her arms around my shoulders.

—If you like I'll take you to places where they initiate you sexually. You can't even imagine what goes on there.

On the landing as I ring for the elevator.

—You can even bring along your little sluts. We'll lick them into shape.

As the elevator descends.

—You shit! You bastard! You'll never ever have me again!

Sitting in comfortable armchairs on either side of the bed that fills the center of the room. I listen to her read me a letter she wrote me but then didn't dare to send.

Merely boring stuff, in the tone of the confessions of a young girl still uncertain regarding love; however, the final few lines, which are in fact what these pages have been aiming to say, quicken my attention.

—It's true what I've written there. Up until five or six days ago I didn't know what an orgasm was. Several times I'd heard the word spoken, but I didn't know what it really meant. I looked for it in the dictionary.

She crumples the letter nervously in her bag.

—There's nothing in the dictionary. I didn't understand a thing. Tell me what an orgasm is.

She steals flowers from the public gardens at night and then places them in pots on her windowsill.

I would love to make you come on order, when I want you to, to make your sex stiffen again even right after an ejaculation, so that it would be impossible for you to leave me, so that you'd have another hard-on without having left my pussy.

On the brink of tears.

—When I realized, I said nothing to anyone. Him, there was no point, he's incapable. Besides, to be truthful, it wasn't his. As for my parents, I wasn't going to tell them the mess I was in. I went there all on my own. It was freezing, I was frozen, I was scared. The doctor and the two nurses who were with him were hateful. I'm sure they hurt me deliberately so that I wouldn't do it again. I know they thought I was a whore. I wanted to die. It was worse than awful. Worse than disgusting. Can you imagine me with a brat? First of all I don't want any kids. Can you see me in a mother's role? My life would be shot, that's what it amounted to. I really believe I've other things to do than bring up a bunch of children. It was a horrible moment. I felt I was up to here in slime, in filth.

As she finishes undressing me she's suddenly at my back, has one arm round my waist while the other hand is sneaking between my thighs.

—Let me jerk you off from behind.

Out of doors, admired, desired, she feels free, happy, invincibly superior.

She would love to "die" during lovemaking, she envisaged it as a form of a sacrifice.

Her room's funereal decor, black satin sheets, the big mirror on the wall reflecting a skull together with the bed.

In a cage set on a pedestal, a white mouse whose incessant nibbling fills the room.

—I start licking slowly, slowly, after that I suck, but still slowly, with me it's not your slam-bang top-speed suck-off. When I'm doing it properly, I want things to go on for a while.

—Take me to a hotel, you'll do to me everything you want. You'd see if you could touch me there that I'm right on the edge. Whatever you like, just ask me. As we walk I can feel it spreading open. Take me there quick.

In her seat on the train, head and shoulders leaning against the glass, her legs spread, in front of where her sex is there is a tiny hole in her trousers into which it is easy to slip the point of the tiny makeup pencil she took from her bag.

A game which at first excites her, then brings her to a state of nervous weeping.

On the telephone: I'm going to say all kinds of things to get you hot, you'll tell me what it's doing to you. I want your cock to get so hard you'll go out of your mind. Now listen. This is my slut's voice.

Midnight strikes somewhere in the town. The wind saws upon the window of the room that she has darkened by draping a scarf over the one lit lamp. The heat weighs heavily.

Seated on the edge of the bed, she knows that I am watching her remove her stockings.

She swallows the sperm that has spurted into her mouth.

—Thank you.

At the door of the taxi that is to take them away she contrives to kiss the young man, all the while keeping her eyes fixed on me. While in his arms, she even lets her hand now and then slide down along her body, one of the fingers of that hand twitching obscenely.

In the afternoon they come over to drink coffee. They are fat. They laugh loudly. They have raucous voices. They are rather frightening and come out with words you don't always understand.

—That dong of his, he can just keep it for himself.

—My ass doesn't belong to him, we don't have a contract.

—First there are the kids that have to be fed, but he turns up and wants it right away.

—They say the youngest is into it already.

—She's just following in her mother's footsteps.

They yuck it up, light cigarettes. They turn toward me, sitting on a chair at the back of the kitchen.

—And him over there, suppose he's got one too?

—It's going to be a while yet, something's not working in there.

I redden. One of them comes over and kisses me.

—Can I touch?

—Touch if you want to, but there's no snap to it at all.

A hand is fiddling with me.

—I jerked him off in the corridor where you exit from the movie theater, his come spattered onto the red carpet. When the audience came out, I watched them walking on it without realizing.

That turned me on, that did.

It was nighttime, I was trailing about in the streets, not knowing what I was looking for, when I came upon a very big man, very tall, very strong. He took me by the arm without a word and drew me into a dark corner. He lifted me up and sat me on a windowsill. He pulled off my panties, tearing them halfway apart in the process, and got right to fucking me as hard as he could. I was pinned against him. It lasted only a few minutes. He left me on my windowsill, after stuffing some money between my thighs.

A black velvet suit. Upon it may be read every detail of her body. When as she walks she extends either leg, you can see the slight form of her garter underneath the material.

—Are you looking at me?

Halted in front of me.

—How would you describe me?

Swaying her hips.

—See my little curls?

Blond fuzz on her neck.

—Aren't I pretty? Am I getting you up?

I'll be as sweet as water from a fountain.

I'm drawing a picture of your sex.

She lights a cigarette and rounding her lips takes a long drag.

—I'm sucking you off.

—*Dick*, to me the word has something so dirty about it that I hardly dare pronounce it. Sometimes while walking alone in the street I repeat it to myself: A *dick*. A big *dick*. Sucking a *dick*. Pulling off a *dick*. It's unbelievable what that does to my nerves.

The metallic sheen of street lighting on women's stockinged legs.

They had dined together with friends. The whole while they were at table she made incessant allusions to bedroom frolics.

As they came out of the restaurant she took his arm, clinging closely to him. Her usual perfume.

—Let's leave the others.

After the good-byes she puts her arm firmly round his waist. It is a mild, humid night.

—I'm inviting you to my place. I've arranged a little apartment, you'll like it.

She quickens her pace a little.

—I live just a couple of streets away.

Her hand descends slowly over his buttocks, finally slipping between his legs.

—I can feel your balls as you walk. Like two little birds.

Her other hand has grasped his sex.

—Now I've got all of you.

She writes:
You want me on my knees.
I'm on my knees.
No matter what happens, I come back to you, tirelessly, always.
Only you fit me.

—He's always getting into a fight with me, he gets angry, but there's no way, I can't make love with him, it's too much, he revolts me.

On the chair beside mine at the café table.

—I like caresses, I like men to be gentle, to talk to me.

Her red lips on the cup's rim.

—He's a brute.

Her way of drinking, falsely elegant, with her little finger in the air.

—He wants it immediately, then it's over. That's not how you give a woman an orgasm.

The cigarette.

—Love, it's something beautiful, something like when you're a child and you're being rocked to sleep.

A long puff on her cigarette.

—Me, I'm willing to go along with whatever anyone asks me, but not like that, not in those conditions, any old how, like animals.

Looking off into space.

—And I hate crude words. For example, he calls it a *cock* or a *dick* or a *tool*. It shocks me.

She again picks up the cigarette she had left in the ashtray.

—*Cock, dick, tool,* those are words I don't like.

Perhaps giving it further thought.

—Especially *cock,* don't you agree?

Her cigarette has gone out.

—I don't know, but if I really had to absolutely make a choice, I think I would prefer *dick,* it's softer, but we could certainly speak of these things some other way, don't you think? Why always *cock, dick,* or *tool?*

Relights her cigarette.

—We would even invent nice words, why not? That's what he can't understand. He's a pig. A great fat pig.

Beautiful white teeth displayed by a smile.

—You understand what I'm saying, don't you?

The hand holding the cigarette trembles imperceptibly.

—That's what I would like to find, precisely. A man who understands me, a man who is sensitive to those things.

The cigarette stubbed out in the ashtray with a kind of rage.

—Because, you know, I like love as much as anyone else, I'm even very hot. I know myself. Very hot. Anyway, I'm a woman but I want to be respected as such.

Another sip of coffee.

—Just let them stop saying *cock* or *dick* or *tool* to me.

The cup is set down a little askew on the saucer.

—When they say *pussy* for a woman, that I can accept. *Pussy*. To me that's a rather cute word. In any case, it's nothing like *dick*.

The hour on her wrist.

—Excuse me, I have to get back to work. It's time. I hope you don't hold it against me for having spoken so frankly to you?

As soon as she's seated in the taxi her hand wriggles its way under the folds of my overcoat, gropes a little before finding my fly, opens it, searching for my sex.

—Well now, let's see what shape we are in today.

A darkened, damp street.

In the recesses of a doorway, young, pretty, fragile in her gray raincoat, its collar turned up over her long hair, she plays with me the game of the whore angling for men passing by.

—Coming along, honey?

A wink.

—I'm so hungry for it I won't even make you pay.

Her hand trailing over me.

—You'll be my last one tonight.

She leads the way toward a hotel nearby.

—My tongue feels thick.

—Yesterday I waited for you.

Insistent voice.

—You promised to come.

Her lip trembles a little.

—Go where you will, I don't care, I'm not jealous, but don't tell me you'll come when you know you aren't going to.

She turns her back as though she had decided to leave, but does not move.

—I know you're with your little whores.

Tears.

—Don't deny it, I saw you.

Her shoulders shaking.

—Filthy little whores, I wouldn't touch them with a stick.

A venomous glare.

—My ass isn't enough for you anymore? My tongue isn't good enough?

A handkerchief between her fingers. Half-whispering.
—Whores, dirty little whores.

A pigeon fallen into the middle of the street, a drop of blood on its beak.

Troubled look of innocence.
Since yesterday I have a new cock.

Heavy lips.

She writes:
I understood that the chain of men was beginning for me, and that each time I had an ever stronger impression that I was losing myself.

Lying adrift on the back of the chair, a narrow hand with long slender fingers.

She is naked, curled up in a big wicker armchair.
—While I dress, you can explain to me how the whores do it. I'll do you just as if I were one. They say that before going to bed with him, they wash the man's cock, is that true?

In the bit of black and white checkered cloth, so short it barely covers her thighs, she pivots graciously in front of the window of the room.

—Do you like it?

My nodded indication that I do.

—I got myself fucked wearing it just before I came.

Voice trails away.

—But he didn't like the skirt.

I wake up.

I think of you.

My bed is nice and warm.

I want your fingers.

I want your hands.

I want to fall asleep from love.

I want your sex planted like a knife in mine.

—I bought a cake.

A turnover she holds between her fingers.

—I'm just going to make a tiny hole in it so I can touch the cream with my tongue.

By slow stages her tongue works itself all the way in between the leaves of pastry.

—Each time I bring back a little more come, it's delicious. Wouldn't you like to take a little bit from my tongue with the tip of yours?

When the piece of pastry is no more than an empty shell.

—I've got it all. I'm really good at sucking.

The shell is put down on the café table.

—You see what would be real bad would be for you to jerk off and fill it up with your come. If you took it with you to the toilet you could do it. You'd bring it back full and I'd start again. If you like I'll come with you and jerk you off. Look at the hole, there's just enough room for the tip of your cock. Only you have to be very careful not to break it when you come.

She manipulates it.

—You like to see me suck like that?

She thrusts her tongue back into the cavity.

—Maybe you'd also like to see me sucking another cock?

Her lips are thick.

—In any case, I know it would do something for me.

I would rent a room in whatever fleabag hotel in a small working-class town and wait for her there, she would arrive as night was falling, climbing the broken stairs, and as she went past in the poorly lit hallway a dangerous-looking, hairy-chested man in a T-shirt would open his door, she felt she was within an inch of being raped by him, she would finally reach our room and no sooner inside, her back against the closed door, would undo the belt of her leather coat under which she would be in stockings and garters and in high heels, I would contemplate her as she took my sex in her mouth before we made love standing in these squalid surroundings.

—In such a place, I could stay excited all the time. You know what would be wonderful?

Her wolflike eyes.

—As soon as we've finished, each of us, I'll go down into the street, you'll follow me, I'll open my coat and the first guy who's interested, I'll let him have me against a wall.

The young lady is tall, dark-haired, always wears scent and makeup.

She takes you in her arms, holds your head tight in her extravagant odor, embraces, kisses, burbles little sweetnesses, then, one day as we're sitting on the edge of the bed, she lowers with precaution the cloth knickers, the little white pants.

—But it's already in lovely form, your little pet-cock. Oh how pretty it is! How I love it! I have to kiss it. Do you mind it I kiss your little pet-cock?

One doesn't understand why, this time, the young lady kisses with the inside of her mouth.

I would like the day to come when you beg me to stop giving you pleasure.

Lying flat on her stomach on the floor, her tight trousers molding her legs and her buttocks, by herself she simulates the movements of lovemaking, her body shuddering, her hips working to the left and to the right.

—Watch me, I'm fucking.

While waiting for my train to pull out, her eyes defying me from the other side of the glass, she begins the act of lifting her clinging black dress in public.

She writes:
On my knees, my hands clasped, I worship your sex, it is my god.

Between two fingers, holding them by their stems above her open mouth, her head tilted back a little, she snapped up the dark red cherries one by one.

Between her lips, her sticky juice-stained tongue: a nervous little animal in its lair.

—I would like to have cocks by the dozen, cocks and balls. I'd play with them and afterward put them away in a box or a drawer.

—Want me to show you the specialties of the house?

Playfully, she bends down, takes my sex between her hands, brings her lips close without touching it and with it near sticks out her tongue. After that, make-believe caresses, a pretended running of the tip of her tongue on the outside and the inside of the ear.

—There's also the little hole, but I can't show you, sir, I do it with my tongue and my little finger, but I'm sure if the gentleman chooses that specialty he will be delighted with me. Moreover, he can take me for anything we offer. I'm very clever and very attentive.

Her face as if aglow with the freshness of youth.

Standing in the middle of the night under the fine rain, her back against the iron grillwork around the park.

She soliloquizes, cigarette between her lips, and now and then utters hoarse cries, grasping her sex in both hands through the material of her dress.

—You see this little string? You need only pull one end of it for my whole bodice to open, right down to my waist.

At the back of the entrance hall of the building, with her two hands the little girl lifts the skirt of her white dress above the hairless mound of her sex, visible as the fine line of a naked slit.

—I would like to make love weltering in blood.

—When I want it, it hurts me right here, in my belly.
A pointed finger almost clinically indicates the spot.

Dressed, she adjusts her body to the mirror, observing herself at length, with her hands caressing the glass, undulating before it with a provocative sensuality that is like a burst of fire.

Flattening her tongue, she licks the glass, a little saliva runs down, she gathers some of it on her fingers and with it darkens the cloth over her sex, which she thrusts at its reflected image, at the same time making a series of obscene faces that, complacent, she watches herself compose, her eyes widening from desire.

—Come and fuck me. You mustn't touch my dress, I want your cock inside it, against my ass, inside me, I'll turn round and you, you'll jam it into my cunt. Look, I'm drooling fuck, my mouth has a hard-on. You'll spray your juice on the mirror, I'll rub my face in it, I'll lick it, I'll swallow it, I love the smell of fuck, I love having it in my mouth.

She stands still, fidgets.

—What do I look like with my hair all messed up like this, all undone, with my face all crazy, my eyes full of cock?

She lifts her arms, stands with her hands applied against the streaks of dribbled saliva, her fingers are spread, her legs are splayed, her feet are bare.

An arrogance in her voice.

—I look like more than a whore, because I am more than a whore.

The gummy mirror at sunrise.

Her stomach bulging a little inside the narrow skirt above the red leather belt round her waist. I think irresistibly of a bee that has heaped its abdomen with gathered pollen.

The smile uncovers the doubtful pink of the gums of her upper jaw. Her unhealthy look gives me an uncomfortable feeling, as though she were performing some involuntary licentious act before me. Under the dark red varnish, the nail of her left little finger is abnormally long. I try to get a glimpse of the other one that she holds bent, her hand resting on her hip. Her shoes are scuffed.

What does she have to say to me? For what reason did she so insist upon paying me a visit?

Sitting across from me, she relates a few anecdotes having to do with her work. Her dream was to become a concert pianist. She likes only *muted* music. She lives alone in a comfortable, very modern apartment. Her friends are interesting, mostly from outside the world of her profession. Like her they are fond of art, books, the theater, films, travel. Recently, she was abroad. She would love to go back there if she had the chance. Am I acquainted with many foreign countries?

Somewhere, from far away, a woman's frightened shriek.

The white material of women's silky lingerie.

A necklace of small pearls.

In the semi-darkness of the street you would think she was emerging from the very walls themselves, becoming suddenly present, a strange apparition, her hand searching an instant for the sex, after that just as suddenly disappearing into an entry whose door she slams shut behind her.

A button of her too-tight bodice pops open to reveal the black brassiere at which the men seated nearby on the terrace cast covert glances.

—I'm depraved, you know.

She laughs.

—I don't know why, it's always this same button that opens. You can see my brassiere, can't you? All the men are looking at me. Men too, they're depraved, every one of them.

Her fingers fiddle unsuccessfully with the troublesome button.

—I like to have men look at me. At night if I'm alone in my bed, I think back on it. I become icy cold and then hot all over.

We'll drive all night. At dawn we'll stop in the first village we come to. There'll be a hotel room with thick eiderdowns, net curtains at the windows, a big bed and antique furniture. There'll be hot coffee with croissants, butter and jam, there'll be my night's exhaustion, I'll lie down fully dressed, you'll lie down beside me, and we'll hold hands without moving, like corpses.

Such a sweet innocent mouth, yet we know what its caresses can be.

Blue coat and toque that turn her into a Russian doll.

The door of the room no sooner shut than she starts to dance with a fascinating sylphlike lightness.

—Does blue suit me?

With a casual gesture she removes the toque and carelessly tosses it over her shoulder, then slips out of the coat, which falls at her feet.

Her dress is red.

—Does red suit me?

The dance quickens as she takes off the dress which flies in the air for a moment before landing softly on the floor.

—Does black suit me?

She hums a little rhythmic tune while moving about on tiptoe as she unhooks her brassiere and whips off her black panties.

—Does nudity suit me?

For an instant she stands still in the liquid light from the big window, then, laughing, lets herself fall across the bed.

She has narrow shoulders, a slender neck, frothy hair,

the face and the body of a child in a short skirt that leaves her black stockinged thighs visible.

Smiling.

—I am meeting people, making acquaintances.

She hops about, sticking out her tongue impishly.

Waiting to cross the street.

—You, I'd like to scratch you, to tear you to pieces, to eat you so that you'd be nobody's but mine.

One of her nails digs into my wrist.

—You're forever trying to get away from me. You talk and what you say never makes any sense at all. With you it's always complicated.

I twist one of her fingers.

—You're hurting me.

A little later on.

—I like you to hurt me.

I have put on my open bodice so you can play some of those games I love.

She takes her bath with a kind of voluptuous languor, her body surrendered, about it a certain somnolence, her features startlingly calm, serene, out of this world.

Her gaze drifts over her naked body, the little patch of dark seaweed floating where her round thighs meet below her sex.

—I no longer even know how many of them I've had. Fifty maybe. In the beginnning I used to count them.

She sits up in the tub.

—Remembering that blows my mind.

Dripping, she gets out of the water, a big white towel thrown over her shoulders, crosses the room barefoot and throws herself onto the night-rumpled bed, her legs raised.

—Think of this. Just of this. Think as hard as you can. My pussy and your cock.

Her eyelids are closed. Her silence is almost religious.

—When I'm all wet like now, I imagine to myself that I have had a bath in fuck.

Her legs open.

—Do you have a good view of me?

Her hands caress the sheet.

—In the morning, I would like to have a flock of men, each with his cock stiff. I'd try them one after another with me still wringing wet, without moving, just to feel their penetration and their spasmodic movements when they begin to come.

The piercing stare of her green eyes.

Her slowly circling finger draws squeaks from the rim of the glass filled with a rose-colored drink.

Three dahlias standing in a glass vase.

42

This morning, while asleep, I made love with you and I felt the sensation of an orgasm.

—One can't explain how it happens. Suddenly, I looked at my pussy and that brought images to my mind. It's like a switch, as though somebody in my depths was pressing the red button. Then I have this need to act, to get out in the streets, to see men, to know I am going to seduce them. Isn't it the same for you with women? Why do you do it? What is it you want? What are you searching for? You're not going to tell me it's just a cunt and a pair of tits? It's something else. It's first the sex that thinks, the head doesn't think till afterward.

—And the heart?

She hugs her bare legs in her arms.

—Don't you find me animal?

She rocks back and forth on her buttocks.

—That's also what men like in me.

—And the heart?

Her body uncoils, snakelike.

—Maybe when I was born my heart dropped down into my pussy. That's where it throbs.

—Love?

Standing in front of me, spreading her sex with the fingers of both hands.

—Look, here's love, little pink lips, all wet inside and with hair all around. Did you get a good look? I can also show you my ass, it too is a little piece of heart and a little piece of love. Now, leave me to myself. It's a magnificent day outside. I am going to get myself up like one hell of a whore and go out in the street and give them erections like you've never seen. Today, I have the feeling I'm going to fuck myself to death.

The newness of her adolescent voice.

—I'll be waiting for you like a good little whore.

It's unanimous, everyone finds her younger than her daughter. She's been told so a hundred times over. They're even the same size, same figure, she wears her clothes. They're regularly taken for sisters. As for men, she's the one they tend to court.

It's true, she has more charm. Her daughter is indeed very pretty, and it's true that she takes after her, but there's something missing, grace maybe, a particular way of being seductive, of being attractive.

Recently, her daughter had a flirt, a little something that really amounted to nothing at all, the way they have them at that age. Very soon she realized that the young man felt something for her. She immediately stopped allowing him inside the house, the situation would have become unbearable. It's her daughter who has a life to make for herself, not she.

I love you. You have to believe me. The men I've

known have been nothing to me. It's with you I want to make love. Love like a communion, like a great sacrificing of my self.

Damp twilight of that windowless room where the heavy wooden bed takes up nearly all the space.

She cries out with pleasure, her body arched. A dog whimpers behind the door.

Wearing an electric blue dress, standing on the step of the passenger car.

—Put your finger up me, fast.

Her sex, wet, leechlike. The finger slips in easily. She gives a little sigh.

Before the automatic door shuts:

—I'll masturbate thinking of you.

Still less distinctly:

—I'll smoke you.

She was short of cigarettes but I learned later that she bummed a few from someone and in that way was able to smoke me during the whole trip.

—In the train my urge for sex was driving me out of my mind. I went into the toilet to get out of my dress and put on a pair of pants because I looked too whorish. Men kept staring at me and I wasn't interested. I just wanted to smoke you, you know how. On arrival I was a little dizzy, I'm not used to tobacco. I was getting wet all on my own, I went to someone I know and asked him to masturbate in front of the mirror. I caught his juice in my hands. I rubbed it until nothing was left. It was still early. I let a guy in the street touch me. It didn't do anything for me. I wanted to get some sleep. I went home. I made myself a hot chocolate and ate cookies, sucking you off as I ate them. First nibbling round the edges, then gobbling it whole. I slept till eleven. I'm calling you from my bed. Can you hear my voice? It's my mouth-full-of-fuck voice, as you say. I'm all bare between my pink sheets, all pretty, with my little pussy real soft and sweet. It would be wonderful if you were here. I'd take you in my arms and we wouldn't budge from here all day, especially as it's raining. I don't like the rain. I need the sun the way I need sex. It's strength. It's life. You've just got to come. I'll sleep until you get here. I'll leave the door open. Just push it and you'll slip into my bed. I won't know who you are. You'll make me put my head on your belly, holding me tight by the neck. My tongue will caress you. Are you coming?

I have my hair up with lots and lots of pins in it so you can play at taking them out and each lock will fall, one by one.

—There are two things about you I don't yet know, your handwriting and what your fuck smells like.

Shelling the peas, she plunges her hands sensuously into the bowl in which they are collecting.

—I have them under my fingers, they're cool and smooth. I imagine them to be a pile of little balls and it excites me.

Stretched out on the bed underneath the weight of her outspread black dress, the intense whiteness of the silk of her garter belt.

The swollen breasts that with a mechanical gesture she lifts out of her brassiere.

—I'm showing them to you, otherwise it would be buying a pig in a poke.

Her thick body inside its ample clothing.

—I'll do you however you like, you've paid, but my real specialty is cock-sucking. I have pepper on my tongue.

The room is warm from the day's sun, the woodwork on it smooth as steel, from behind the shutters one can hear an indefinable murmur of voices.

At night you make love to other women. You come, and the thought of that is terrible for me.

Early in the morning, in the café near the station where she has just found me, wearing a short multicolored skirt and a spotless blouse. She curls up beside me on the long banquette.

—I'm dressed up as a little girl, isn't that what you like?

So fresh, so innocent does she indeed appear that one could crush her with tenderness in one's arms.

—When I woke at my parents' house this morning, I thought about going to see you today and right away I wanted to jerk you off.

Her hand posed on my sex, which she begins to caress with her little fingers spread out like a fan that suddenly closes when that hand slips between my thighs, where she keeps it, even when the waitress arrives.

—Do you think that she, too, has toyed with someone's balls this morning?

I shall be a tightrope stretched out for you.

With me in an office where I am at work she straddles a chair and discreetly rubs herself against its back, with a glance of complicity in my direction.

I am made for love.

Slow suppleness of the thick hair with faint golden reflections.

A man's shirt, boots, a cap, and a pair of big earrings.

—Take me to some really disgusting place where there'll be rusty old iron clinkers, and lots of nasty bugs. You'll lay me down in the middle of all those horrors and I will make love to you.

Elegantly dressed in a black suit, with a reddish brown silk shirt whose straight collar sets off the lower part of her face.

She writes:

Naked to the waist I am writing to you. I'm holding this pen the way I would a big strong cock. You ejaculate fuck ink. Keep some back my love. The night is long and I am here. Have you guessed what awaits you?—enormous gouts of my pleasure upon the hairs of your sex.

Every time we pass in front of her house on our way back from school or errands, she dashes out holding her dress up, laughing loudly, showing off a long pair of split pantaloons decorated with lace.

—Discharging. An odd word, but it gets me off. More so than juicing.

Her cheek lies amidst the waves of her hair on the white bolster.

—I love all love's words, don't you?

Slenderness of her arm all the way to the shoulder.

—Who invented these words? The first time I heard *cock* I must have been ten or eleven, and someone had taken me into a café, I needed to do pipi, to go to the toilet, and there were men in there talking together. Maybe because of the men and the odor I understood it was connected with sex. The other words, men I've known have taught them to me. For example, *hand-job* instead of *masturbating*. That's an expression that really gets me going. *Hand-job* is hard, crude. Every time, I imagine a swollen cock getting a good polishing.

Sucking on a lock of her hair.

—Do those words excite you too? With me they go in deep below my skin, they trouble me, they cause a commotion inside me, I lose my bearings. I turn into another woman, a little demon.

—You have drops of fuck on your pants.

With that she sticks out her tongue.

—Come here, I'll lick them off.

Without charm, having plain features, dry lackluster hair.

She is reading a thick book, but from time to time she glances round the little café where there is no one apart from ourselves.

Proceeding with ostentation, she lays her book upon

the table, pushing this aside enables her to slide along the wall that is faced with a mirror in which she does not fail to stare at me as she heads toward the toilets.

There she waits a long time for me to join her.

Back in the room, she pulls a little blue purse from her bag and picks out, coin by coin, the price of her drink. She picks up her book, which she keeps in her hand, and moves at a lively pace toward the door, passing as close as possible to my table.

—You don't know what you missed.

She goes out and, on the sidewalk, melts into the crowd.

I go to sleep sniffing my panties. I was already doing that when I was a little girl.

Young and happy she frolics ahead in front of me in the hallway of the big hotel where we have just arrived, holding her skirt up at waist height.

—You can't imagine how I'm longing to have you in my mouth. That's all I've been thinking of since a few minutes ago.

She lets go of her skirt and turns round.

—Do you find me pretty?

—Yes.

—Very pretty?

—Yes.

Her arms behind her head, her hands gripping the thick mass of her hair.

—And very exciting?

—Yes.

—Say it.

—Very exciting.

Leaning back against the wall, one leg bent at the knee.

—And very whorish?

—Yes.

—Say it.

—Very whorish.

Hugging my arm with both of hers, her head resting on my chest.

—The biggest whore you've ever known, that's what I'd like to be.

The vacant beach, its dead colors.

To be everywhere with you for making love.

Under the escort of two elderly women a troop of children wearing blue and white uniforms passes down the street, each one of the little girls casting a long glance in her direction.

Wearing a see-through dress, she was entering the room from the big terrace it adjoined.

Before the shape of her body within the stirrings of the cloth, a shape revealed by the dazzling back-lighting, one's gaze is riveted upon that sensuality offering itself to rape, one held one's breath, one's heart gripped in the visceral confusion of temptation.

After having evoked a little of her recent past, that troubled period of her first youthful years, her features contracted, almost in tears:

—Let's not talk any more about it, it's sordid.

She's learning that there is a price to pay for everything.

—Why isn't life always as beautiful as it is tonight?

Only later will she realize the exact value of the moment that she had lived as in a dream within this calm and magnificent garden setting.

She draws the curtains on the corridor side of the empty compartment, kicks off her shoes, and climbs on her knees up onto the seat, looks at herself in the mirror above it, smiles at me, starts humming, uncovers a pair of satin panties.

—I bought them yesterday. No one has seen them yet. I put them on on purpose for you.

Doing some parody bumps and grinds.

—When you're with me you've got to have a hard-on all the time.

She turns round, leaps over in one bound to the side where I am sitting.

—First of all, how's your cock?

Her hand.

—Maybe it's hard for someone else?

Her head on my lap.

—I would like to know all the women you have fucked.

She takes one of my fingers into her mouth, licks it along its entire length.

I look at you, I touch you.

—Hey there, dearie, you got to get a move on, I've other things to do.

Her manner is abrupt, her eyes indistinct behind thick lenses.

—Have you lost your juice or something?

Her voice is harsh.

—Either you let me have it fast or you get out of there.

Her chin is pointed.

—If you don't get off faster than that at your age, you're not going to be around for long, believe me, it's a whore who's telling you.

She pulls her stockings up over her skinny thighs.

—Try frigging yourself tonight, maybe that'll work for you.

Fully dressed.

—Okay, get your ass out of here, I want to have a little pee.

The hotel stairway smells of boiled fish.

—I get it out of their pants and immediately begin to lick the end until it becomes nice and hard and long. Then I suck it. The balls are off there at the back. I go after them like this.

Agile movements of her outstretched tongue, her hand closing upon invisible roundnesses.

—What I like is to scratch them from underneath.

The ends of her fingers curl into hooks.

—See how I do it to them?

Observing the women as they move hither and thither with the crowd.

—Which one would you pick for fucking out of all those?

A well-dressed young lady with a somewhat severe expression.

—I bet she's never yet set eyes on a cock.

A woman moving along with short quick steps.

—You told me that women who walk with their legs pressed together that way don't like being fucked. You think it would be fun to try?

A rather pretty woman leaning on a man's arm.

—That one, she has her cock but she hasn't got yours.

Grabbing hold of me, dragging me off, forcing me almost to run.

—I'm the one who's got yours! . . . It's me who's got yours! . . .

Very light blue eyes in a very sweet round young face.

She crouches down in front of me in the public park, underneath the pleated blue skirt her thighs are sufficiently spread for me to be able to see the tight crotch of the white panties.

Hers is the smile of a little girl who wishes not to be forgotten.

Her body open as though from having been cast adrift, from having gone under.

—Fuck me! Fuck me! My husband is hopeless!

Wild laughter.

—It's as if you were fucking him, that asshole!

Hard arms round my waist, bands of iron.

—Fuck me, stuff me, let it demolish him, that good-for-nothing!

She goes running up the stairs in front of me, then stands still on the landing while I continue to climb, the roundness of her young thighs visible up to her panties beneath the billowing white petticoat.

Her face half-buried in the pillow of the bed she is stretched out upon.

—I'm a poor little abandoned child, sir, a poor little lost orphan.

Seemingly on the verge of tears.

—Wouldn't you be willing to adopt me? You are rich, sir, and you don't have a little girl. Adopt me, please adopt me. You'll see how grateful I'll be, how nicely I'll suck you off.

—I only know *cock, pecker, prick, penis, dick, tool, dong, member, schlong, weenie, wang, sausage, stick,* do you know any others?

Organ music from a nearby church.

Little fingernails with rounded tips.

She is all alone on the station platform waiting for me, unforgettably pretty, her hair drawn back under a man's light gray fedora, a note at once elegant and equivocal underscored by the man's jacket and a pair of tight-cut trousers that lengthen her legs, in her hand a rose which she extends to me with a gesture of deliberate graciousness, a smile in her eyes.

Something fairylike about this as though otherworldly instant.

I would like to move about for you, naked, to dance

for you and then to be taken by you, wet with perspiration, hot with sex, an arrogant whore.

Mouthing the neck of a bottle of mineral water.
—There are times when I would suck anything.

—When I was a little girl I couldn't stand contact with my mother's skin.

—You have a lot of sperm, it's good. I am going to keep it on my tongue for a long time.

—It was you who taught me the name of touch-me-nots and that they smell good at night. I always keep a pot of them on my windowsill. I look at them in the summer and I think of you.

Shocked, rigid, her features drawn.
—I saw her die, it's disgusting.
The pallor of her cheeks.
—Death is disgusting.
Her head against my shoulder, her arms round my neck.
—Tell me I'll never die. That I will always be young and pretty, always desirable.

Holding me tight.

—What do you have to do to not die?

One inside the other, suddenly in tears.

—As soon as we have finished you'll go away, we'll
have done everything as though we loved each other, but
we won't love each other, and I'll be alone once again, like
when you found me on the street, with men, it's love I'm
looking for, for there to be one who'll take me to his home
and every day we'll do things together, so that it has a
meaning, what meaning does it have that you be inside
me with your sex, five minutes ago I didn't even know
you, you take me in your arms as if you loved me and it
isn't true, you hardly even looked at me beforehand, you
don't know how I'm shaped, all you care about is to fuck
me, to add another girl to your list, that's enough for you,
you are rotten, all of you, I told myself that if I wasn't
married by the time I was thirty, if I hadn't managed to
have a home by then, I was never going to fuck again, I
shan't miss it, I've had enough, I'm fed to the teeth on the
dirty stuff they have never thought twice about doing
with me.

—Are you undressing me?
—I'm undressing you.
—How are you undressing me?
—The shoes.
—Then?

59

—The dress.

—Underneath it I have a silk blouse.

—The stockings.

—The garter belt.

—No.

—I knew it.

—After that?

—You keep your brassiere on too.

—No. We take it off.

—We take it off.

—The silk blouse, the panties, and the garter belt are left.

—We don't touch anything after that.

—All right. We don't touch anything after that.

Her hands haven't ceased their irritating flutterings at just about the level of her face, coated with desire.

—We're taking a taxi?

—In the taxi I don't want you to touch me.

—You, you can touch me.

—Maybe my feet will hurt.

—I'll take care of them in the room.

Her pure girlish smile.

—Could I take off my blouse, just to shock the driver?

—Won't you be naked?

—Except for the panties and the garters.

She lies down beside me.

—Someday we must do it for real.

She's fat, her yellow dress is too short, and you can see her polka-dot panties.

—Why don't you ever want to play with me?

No boy ever wants to play with her.

—I'm a game you don't know.

Some of her front teeth are missing.

—Let's go over there toward the toilets.

She pulls me by my shirt.

—You don't have to do anything, just lie down on the ground on your back.

Stretched out, I see her get out of her panties and then come to place herself, with her legs apart, right above my head.

—Don't move at all, that's the game.

A hot flood splashes upon my face.

A good lollipop, ah, that's what I like!

She licks her lips in anticipation.

Back from the fair.

—I took a ride in the bumper cars. There was this big guy, he was out of control, wouldn't stop banging me really hard.

Trousers and a red pullover.

She is crazy about shoes and spends hours contemplating them in shop windows without, most often, being in a position to buy the ones she fancies.

—The foot, you know, it's love.

Her legs crossed, she is swinging one of hers.

—If you caress my feet I become electric.

It was the evening, it was already dark, for a long time he had followed me in the street, he didn't dare to speak to me, I could feel him behind me, it was exciting me, suddenly I turned round, I pushed him up against the wall, I opened his fly, I stroked his cock, I crouched down in order to suck it and left him like that, I ran off laughing, I was wet.

His hand on mine.

—Where shall we go?

—To our café. You can eat cakes.

Joyous.

—Yes, yes, yes, oh I want to! We'll sit at the back table, on the banquette that curves, nobody can see us there, I'll take cream cakes and smear cream on your cock and lick it off after, I'll put some in my cunt too, I put a little in there every day, it does something for me.

She wanted to know whether I had already made love in a confessional, maybe she wouldn't dare, it would depend, if someone shoved her in there and took her without giving her any time to think about it, just the time for a bang, she wouldn't be against that, but afterward she believes she would have to confess, and to know there'd be a priest sitting right next to the spot where she had fucked, that would make her hysterical, had I already known a hysterical woman? is it true that you can calm them down simply by fucking them? didn't they use to say that those women were possessed? and yet it's just a sickness like any other, nymphomania too, but no one wants to know she's a nymphomaniac, you don't talk about it, you hide it, when you get yourself a man you don't think about it and so you see how one might argue that every woman that fucks is a nymphomanic, that desires are stronger in some than in others, what does that prove?

—I drive in my car into the outlying sections. First I drive around two or three times to make sure I've been noticed. Bodywork like my car's can't go unnoticed. The kids come flocking. I only keep the ones who're thirteen or fourteen. I have them get in the back and masturbate for me if they want to earn the brand-new banknote I wave under their noses and that I finally glue to their stiff little cocks with a dab of their own scum. When it's over I absolutely have to fuck, I can't stand another minute without it, I pick up the first cock that's wandering around.

Lying back on the stairs in the hotel corridor while on the floor above a lively discussion between women can be heard, she spreads her legs only very slightly. Her panties are a scarlet streak in the roiling depths.

—You know how many I've had today?
Her eyes are slits. The tip of her tongue appears.
—Twenty.
She laughs, leaning her head on her shoulder, her mouth wide open.
—And I sucked them all.

To see you naked, with your cock erect, my eyes would overflow with enjoyment.

At thirty, if I haven't achieved what I want, either I'll commit suicide or I'll become a prostitute.

—I dreamt a cat was scratching me. It scared me. Cuddling up.
—No matter what I do, inside me I'll always be a little girl. You must be able to understand that.

—I was with him, we went into every building on the street for a few minutes, just long enough for me to suck him a bit behind each door. We'd said he'd only come when we got to the last one. I kept it in my mouth, rolling it from right to left, fat cheeks, I saw a cop, I went to ask him for some directions, I swallowed it all just before speaking to him.
Her laugh is that of a child who has just performed a practical joke.

—I've written something. Do you want me to read it to you?

With its gilding, its tapestries, its little pieces of inlaid furniture, its subdued lighting, the room is snug against the night.

From a traveling bag she draws an exercise book and sits down beside the bed upon which I am stretched out.

—Are you listening?

She crosses her knees and the light causes sparkles here and there on the scintillating material of her stockings. Her blond hair swept up at her temples, her profile with its sensual lips, her skin a delicate pink.

—It's something I wrote down one night, you know, just like that.

The book is open on her knees.

—Let me begin.

She leans slightly forward in order to see better.

—If you don't like it, you tell me.

She reads.

—After fucking, I feel sickened by him, I don't know who he is, he picked me up in the street, I followed him to the hotel, anyway, he's a disgusting creep, he fucks like a disgusting creep, I look at him sprawled on the bed with his arms folded behind his head, he looks like a fat swollen rat, his cock is soft, floppy, I wonder how I could've sucked that thing, I want to vomit on him, he has got to know what I feel, I must insult him.

A child's face.

—Butt-fucked toad, old whore, white discharge, clapped-up cock, piss, asshole, cheesy, gluey hairs, cunt juice, motherfucker, spit, great big piece of shit, garbage, shithouse runoff, rat's juice, shit juice, garbage juice, poxy pussy juice, black juice, buggered juice, old slut's juice, fuckface, fuck, fuck, fuck . . .

Around us the bedroom is a fetal envelope.

She writes:

It's one in the morning. My parents have just left. A bath is running. Soap me. On the floor is a pile of white silk for you. You have me eroticized to death. Only when your eyes set upon me do I really exist. I belong to you.

They have been together for about ten years, but their marriage became strained very early on. She claims that for a long time she has had no sexual relations with her husband because whenever she does they conclude for her in a malaise she doesn't dare speak of.

Her parents would disapprove of her divorcing, her husband himself would be against it, not out of love or tenderness, but purely out of convention. It is true that in the company where he holds an important position any such solution would be viewed disfavorably.

All her friends are in fact her husband's friends too, he has cunningly managed to keep at a distance from her anyone who maintains no relations with him. She has no children. She feels lonely, that her life is going to waste.

Her last hope would be some lucky encounter that would bring her some moral security and, at the same time, some affection, for at her age, over thirty, the love she dreamt of as an adolescent is something about which she has no more illusions.

—I've quite ruled that out.

She kneads her handkerchief.

—And so, yes, sometimes I go out and walk the street, like a whore, and choose one who doesn't look too bad.

She shakes her head.

—It's awful.

Weak, her complexion faded, she lies in bed propped up by pillows.

—Please shut the door, then at least we won't have my husband in here with us.

She throws back the sheet and the blanket. She's wearing a pair of white knickers under a nightgown that she quickly lifts.

—They've taken it all out. You can hardly see it. Look. There's only a tiny scar. They told me it will disappear entirely with time. I was in so much pain during these last weeks that one day I suddenly decided to have it done.

Smiling.

—In one sense it's a good thing. There's nothing I need fear anymore. You can come inside me now, no problem.

—I'm not very beautiful, yet men choose me more often than others I find ten times better looking than I am. I don't know what attracts them. I think they can tell that I am crazy about it, I do it for the money too, of course, but it's above all for the pleasure. At night, it makes me feel good when I've picked up loads during the day. Normally I get to it by about midday, but often I start before then just to calm the yearning I have. What I like is the going upstairs with them, when I can feel them behind me, watching me. I put myself in their place, I imagine what they're thinking, I wonder what their cocks'll be like, what they're going to want. It prickles all round my pussy.

One meets her endlessly in the hotel corridors wearing the strict uniform of a housemaid.

—Is there nothing monsieur is in need of?

Several times she goes back to smoothing her eyebrows with a finger.

In tears in the street the little girl screams, her crossed hands pressing down over her dress between her thighs.

Dark jacket and skirt, moving silhouette.

Big raindrops begin to fall. She looks up at the sky, shakes her head like an animal, starts to run, soon disappears.

Because while walking I have slipped my hand inside the waist of my trousers in order to adjust my shirt.

—You're touching them!

She forces herself to walk at my speed.

—We ought to be allowed to caress each other in the street.

By and by.

—It's made me want to. Come over here in the corner, I am going to play with them for you.

Open-toed purple shoes.

—Toes have something indecent about them.

Observing her own.

—I never paint them. I leave them as they are, sort of naked, that way I have the feeling they're readier for making love to.

—A tonguing like you're giving me, it's okay, but it's never really anything but kid stuff.

She closes her coat.

—What I'd like is to do it in a bed, that would be something else. Seeing it dripping off your tongue and all.

It's cold weather. On the other side of the big window's net curtain the light is a metallic flatness.

Spacious, beautiful, the room seems lodged within an enclave of somnolence.

Dressed in black clothes, she contemplates herself in the vanity table mirror.

—I'm very pale.

She leans closer to the mirror.

—I didn't sleep last night.

Two fingers follow the underside of her eyes.

—Last night I had a rendezvous. I'd told myself I'd go home around midnight. In fact it was over earlier. It didn't come off. It was someone who'd been trying for weeks. I had him running around for nothing. I don't know exactly what he was after. I didn't even reach for his cock, but even so it had got to me, I needed one, I went into several cafés. Finally I found one in a bookshop that's open at night. He was poking about the books, I was too, he looked just a bit mad, our glances met and I knew it was on. We got started in his car, later on we took a room. I don't know what was wrong with me, it excited me as usual, but it wasn't working with him, I didn't want anything, above all I didn't want him to touch me. He did it to himself there in front of me. I went out into the streets. There was almost no one left. I was hunting for cock. I was becoming hysterical. I went up to a friend's place. He was the one who relieved me. He didn't want me to leave but I was supposed to see you.

The look in her eyes as she slowly raises the laden fork to her mouth and sucks in what had been upon it, then licks her lips after withdrawing it.

I need to fill myself up with you.

The room's window open onto the heat of the night.

—I'm a little cat. A tiny little cat. Put me in the pocket of your trousers so that I keep nice and warm. Down by your balls, it's always warm there. I'll be your little balls-cat.

An ample flower pattern dress, tight-fitting above the waist, her breasts are molded, compacted. She has the elegance and the simplicity of mindless youth.

She is ahead of me, running along the garden's pathways, then stops and plants herself with her back against a tree and stands rubbing her hands slowly one against the other as in a long caress. Glints of light from her half-closed eyes.

She plants her feet apart, leaving one to suppose exactly where her legs come together inside the cloth. Naked, she would be obscene.

She smiles, sticks out her tongue, making it tremble on the edge of her lips, leans her head to one side. She refuses to be approached any nearer, everything must happen at the distance she determines.

A few people are strolling along the gold-speckled pathways.

—This is where I live. It's not very luxurious, but little by little I'm managing to make it nice. When I can I buy something beautiful, or someone gives it to me as a gift.

Her dignity is touching.

—One day I would like to live in a big, big house filled with objets d'art, beauty everywhere, in every room, I love beauty. The world is too ugly. I shall fight to have that house. I'll make a dream house of it.

Kissing my hand.

—I'll invite you. To receive you I'll dress up so well I'll dazzle you. Afterward, I'll do my whore act.

Her cheeks wet with tears.

—Who could I talk to about it?

She looks for a handkerchief.

—I was terribly afraid. It may have been the worst moment in my life.

She dabs at her eyes.

—I was probably idiotic, but when a girl has not been forewarned, I can tell you it turns you upside down. I was also afraid of being damned, as though I had done something evil, as though I had committed a sacrilege. I was sure it was the devil that had got into me, that's what they had taught us at catechism. Everything was mixed up in my mind.

A timid smile.

—To see blood suddenly coming out of you without knowing why, it's horrible.

She blows her nose.

—I don't know why I'm telling you this, I guess because we were talking about my life.

Her hand in her hair.

—Later it was my husband. The first time I had my

period with him he made fun of me. I didn't understand why. I looked at him as though he were a monster.

She sighs.

—And to top the whole thing off, he wanted us to make love. I said no. He slapped my face and tried to force me. I fought back. Naturally, he was the stronger one. He ripped off my pad and started dancing around the kitchen with it. Finally he let me be, but I was in pieces, I felt ashamed and hurt everywhere, if I could have killed myself there and then I would have done it.

She looks at me.

—I shouldn't tell you all this, I don't think I've ever told it to anyone.

Automobile traffic can be heard outside, passing trucks rattle the windows while, nearer by, rough men's harsh voices rise from time to time without it being possible to catch what they are saying in almost angry tones.

Active on top of me in the dark, rather unclean room, for a second she interrupts what she is doing, looks up with an expression of great seriousness, and says in an almost menacing tone:

—When it comes, warn me, I don't take it in my mouth, it's like smoke, I gag on it.

She writes:

My weakness resides in the fact that I am like a wounded animal and that I need love.

Morning quiet in the park where, bathing in gold dust from the sun, she parades for me, moving with the bearing of a queen, the delicate loveliness of her face oddly accentuated by a pair of dark glasses which add to it an enriching, mysterious touch.

We advance in silence, surrounded by the splendor of the flower beds.

A voice that is no longer hers, deep, cavernous, dull, upsetting.

—I want to scratch. I want to bite. I want to spit. I want to tear sexes loose. I'm a devil.

Still hanging on to me.

—Do you realize that I'm a devil?

A banquette at the café. She has a large yellow scarf round her neck. She's sitting with her skirt pulled all the way up to her sex.

—What are you looking at?

—Your thighs.

Gray stockings ornamented with raised black patterns.

—Another half-inch and you can see my panties.

Her eyes lowered, she contemplates herself with lust.

—I'm really a piece, aren't I?

Caressing my arm.

—You know what I've done since the last time we saw each other?

Her fingers seek to twine themselves with mine.

—I've sucked cock like I was crazy.

Young, she married someone high up in the police, but he had sexual requirements that a decent woman cannot tolerate.

After the divorce she met a dental surgeon, very much of a ladies' man, very considerate, unfortunately with a wife and children, and owing to his profession he was rarely free.

She was not yet twenty-eight when she came to believe that her life as a woman was over, she no longer looked for anyone, she had ceased to hope, yet this was when she met the elderly gentleman, always neat and clean, always well-dressed, who is so generous with her without asking much in return, simply to be licked between his thighs from behind, but only once or twice a month, no more than that.

—There's a telephone booth, in there I'll suck you off, no one will see us, I've done it several times before. You suck and you know there are people going by without suspecting anything. You, you'll pretend to be on the telephone, you can say stuff to me to excite me. Do you have a big cock?

—Wintertime, it's like death.

Her dark eyes are drowsy. She hugs herself.

—I don't want to see anybody. I want shuttered, cozily heated bedrooms.

Frozen, immobile.

—Make love to me, let me come back to life.

Morning arises to honor your sex.

All but glued to me in the street at the taxi stand, she picks up the tip of my tie between her fingers and gives little sucks on it, her lips slack.

At night, thirst for your sex, thirst to have your fingers in my body, thirst to suck you till I've drunk you down to the last drop.

—You are how old?
—Thirteen.
—Do you think I'm pretty?
—Yes.
—I've often noticed you looking at me.
—Yes.
—Maybe you thought I didn't see you, right?
—I don't know.
—What were you looking at?
—You.
—Don't play the little innocent. What were you looking at? My legs or my ass?
—I don't know.

—Did you masturbate thinking about me?

—Yes.

—Often?

—Yes.

—How often?

—I don't know.

—Ten times?

—Maybe.

—Smutty little fellow. Did you find me older or less old than your mother?

—Less.

—You've jerked off thinking about your mother?

—No.

—But you jerked off over me?

—Yes.

—Do you already have juice in that little weewee of yours?

—Yes.

—Have you already got up on top of a woman?

—No.

—Never?

—No.

—Fibber. Go shut the door, so we won't be disturbed. That little weewee, I hope it's stiff now?

—Yes.

—Hurry up, I'll get it out for you. It's clean at least?

—Yes.

—Anyway, I couldn't care less. Here, let me do it. Oh! It's true it's already big, this nasty old thing of yours!

—I don't know.

—Are you ashamed?

—No.

—You're not afraid, not at all?

—No.

—Can you feel how nicely I stroke it?

—Yes.

—You know why they call it my little redhead?

—No.

—Because it's red, of course! You want to look?

—Yes.

—Lift up my skirt, I haven't any panties on. Do you like it?

—Yes.

—Before putting your weewee in there you're going to suck it. Do you know how?

—No.

—It's easy. Get down on your knees, bring your mouth up close and lick it well. Inside and outside. You'll see, it's salty.

A black bird motionless on the ridge of the roof.

Her bare arms in the short sleeves of her dress still have that plump roundness of childhood.

A voice with velvet intonations.

There are two of them, sitting on chairs in the park.

—We don't do anything except together.

The second nods.

—Let's agree on how it'll be. You tell us what you want, that way we see what there is to do, because, you know, there're some men, what they ask for, it can make you sick to your stomach. You wonder how they even dare to suggest these things to women.

They introduce themselves.

—That's my sister.

—My sister is a year older than me.

—My sister sucks cock, mainly.

—My sister too.

—They've always said it's you that does it best.

—My sister is good at doing it sitting on a table.

—But we don't want any extra sort of stuff.

—My sister and me, we do it normal-like.

In the direction of the hotel.

—And you'll see, my sister is in white, and me, I'm in black.

In the bath she lets herself have her hair washed and dressed like a child.

The elevator door opens onto a wide thickly carpeted corridor. She precedes me.

—It might be fun being a chambermaid in a hotel like

this one. I'd be the chambermaid of all the single rooms where there would be a man all by himself.

Hopping on one foot.

—Unless the women too think that I'm cute.

Stopping.

—Do I have panties on or do I not? Guess.

—When I have done plenty of fucking on all sides, when I've had all the men I want, maybe I'll enter a convent. Can you imagine me as Saint Whore? In there I'd probably be able to get them all excited too. You, you think there are any who have never set eyes on a cock? If I found a pretty one I don't think I'd mind sucking her, it would be a change from cocks. In any case, it's not due to happen tomorrow, I'm much too fond of men. If I know there's a particular cock that's suffering for me, it gets me all over, I go out of my mind, I have to have it. Just five minutes maybe, but at least I'll have had it, put it up me. Do you think there are women who can do without them? If I didn't have any, I'd take anything instead. The other day I sucked a bicycle pump. An old bicycle pump I found at home in a closet. I also pumped myself. The air, it did sort of tickle me up, but it didn't get me off.

A few steps from the room which has been allocated to us, suddenly, clinging to my arm, halfway embarassed:

—You mustn't pay attention, I've put on a pair of my husband's undershorts.

The so sweetly rounded line of the chin.

—Sometimes in the street, or elsewhere, I just want to give way to tears, so painful is it for me to be stared at. There's hatred on the part of both men and women and, in some men, a desire to debase me with their sex.

—Do you want me to undress again?

—I walk in front of you, you watch me and imagine that I'm making love.

The afternoon sun was burning hot. On the platform she was waiting impatiently for a train.

Kneeling down on the carpet, the game board deployed in front of her.
—One, two, three, four. My pussy's wet.
She throws the dice.
—One, two, three, four, five, six. Looking for a cock.
The dice.
—One, two, three, four, five. I've got a cock.
The dice.
—One, two, three. I shove it in.
The dice.

—One, two, three, four, five. I get it to come.

The dice.

—One, two, three, four. Pussy's calling for more.

She writes:

It's winter. Let me be your blanket. You have to be warm everywhere, hot all over. Come here. I'll give you my little white eiderdown cover to keep your little bells warm.

I'll waft little words over your cock and all these little wafted words will lift it.

I want to sodomize your ears with my little fingers.

I'll blow into your little asshole too in order that the breath of my soul penetrate your body, and into it I'll put my little finger as well, wetted by you. It's so tiny you won't feel a thing. I'll leave it there so as to be with you always.

Sounds of trains passing in the night. She sleeps beside me.

Singing half to herself in the bathroom:

—I had a good fuck . . . I've had my cock . . .

Thin, with copper-colored hair.

She spits methodically into the gutter as she proceeds along the sidewalk. Shut up within herself, she seems oblivious to those around her, completely wrapped up in her strange occupation.

In the moving car.

—I want each man I go with to teach me something. You, what are you going to teach me?

In her vaporous dress, immobile in the middle of the big stairway crowded with hurrying passersby, she is agitating her fingertips, a feverish movement which could as easily be one of beckoning as of some unrelenting caress.

She is smiling, sure of her irresistible sensual power.

Her voice is a soft gasping.

—Come.

The station, in a new black suit made of light material, upon each shoulder a little ladderlike insert through whose open intervals white skin shows.

On my arm.

—Have you seen my little holes?

Going toward the exit.

—Wouldn't you like to stick the tip of your tongue into them?

Heavy rain scarifying the air.

—In material such as this, I always feel like a whore.

The taxi.

—I'm all in black. The underthings too.

Her thigh grazes mine. She hastily draws it away.

—I don't want us to touch until the hotel.

She looks out of the window.

—I was waiting for you at the station for more than an hour. I arrived there ahead of time on purpose, in order to think about you, to prepare myself well. All the men were watching me. I'm sure there are some who took me for a whore.

Her lips are devoid of makeup.

—I thought about your cock. Of the ones I'd sucked in the course of the week. I've had four. Your train was late. My nerves were on edge. If you hadn't come I would have latched onto the first one I ran into. A cock. That's all.

The taxi stops.

—Did you see on the roof of the car? A little bird with a bright yellow head. How pretty it was!

Are you with me in my soul?

Me too, when I was fifteen, I wanted to live a great love affair, a great passion, I'd filled my head with literary models, I imagined myself wearing magnificent white dresses to go dancing beneath the chandeliers with an elegant partner who would be in love with me, who would take me elsewhere, to lakes, mountains, forests where it would be so cold he would have to cover me with furs inside which I would be as if buried, the seashore, the long beaches, I would stay naked from morning till night, my body soaked with the sun, we would have made love in the most beautiful hotels and I would have been capable of dying for him, yes, unfortunately there was real life, he, that sad character, the first time he took me to a dirty little room his relatives were lending to him, the two of us were young, he let me get undressed alone in one corner while he did the same in another, we lay down, I could smell his socks there next to the bed, he climbed on top of me right away, I believe he was already halfway hard, he knew nothing about anything, suddenly there it was in me, he was pushing it inside me, it left me completely cold, he was going up and down as though he was on a rocking horse, he was ridiculous, he was pale, he didn't say a word, I lay still, I still felt nothing, I was afraid he would hurt me, suddenly he collapsed on me like a tire with a puncture, he got out of bed and dressed, telling me that I should hurry, his relatives might arrive at any moment, the whole thing hadn't lasted ten minutes, I wanted to wash but there was no hot water and I only found one dirty towel, I asked him if he had slept with other women, he didn't answer, since he claimed that he loved me we went on with it for two years, a day came when I felt I was suffocating, my life was so sordid, I slept with a man who was older than me, it was just about the same except that he talked to me and showed some tenderness, I had to sleep with several men before understanding that it was me who wasn't working right and that I should forget my adolescent's dreams, now I'm nothing. I just hang out, I go where the wind blows me.

The old lady in black urinates standing in the street.

Halfway smiling, her hair floating about her at once worn and innocent face:

—I'm a vagabond.

In an armchair, her long skirt drawn high over thighs sheathed in net stockings, she puffs mechanically on the cigarette I lit for her, her gaze suddenly clouding.

—Take me in your arms, hold me tight, kiss me.

The giddiness that goes with her wealth and her exceptional beauty.

—We fuck all night and in the morning you strangle me—all right?

She slides open the window onto the balcony from where one has a view over the mist-shrouded city.

—I know you'll never do it. Come stand beside me. They say that city air has a stench. Here, in the morning it has an odor of hazelnuts. Can you smell it?

Her lace dishabille.

—I know someone who would be capable of doing it but he's a eunuch. I mean a real eunuch, I'm not kidding.

Shutting her eyes, she stretches her arms above her head.

—I wish for something like that. That one day I'll be found dead, naked on my bed. You know you always hear that the inquest revealed traces of sperm on the sheets. I would like for it to be on my tongue.

Her dress buttons down the front.

—If you like, I'll unbutton it down to the waist and go out in the street with you like that. Like the whores do.

—Whores don't do that.

—If I were a whore I'd do it. Can you imagine, my garter belt, my panties, and my stockings, all black, in that red dress opening at each step, do you realize how many cocks I'd arouse and the state it would put me in?

The temptress.

—In the street, if I were a whore, would you choose me?

Coming out of a church.

—Me too, I could have washed his feet, even licked them, I've already done that for lots of men, it excites me to caress their feet, me too, I've dried them with my hair. When I do that, I feel exquisitely perverse. It's like nails clawing me along my thighs and down my back.

—Don't talk to me about growing old. I don't care about it. As long as I'm with you and we have a terrific life. I know some who aren't even half your age and yet they're like stiffs alongside of you. Then I want you to teach me, I want us to do things together. Provided I give you a hard-on, the rest doesn't count.

I'm totally in pieces.

—I didn't care for my grandfather. When he died, the family was surprised that I would want to stay alone with him for a while at the undertaker's.

Her face is drawn, her dark eyes sunken.

—I don't know how it came to me. The night before I had thought so much about his prick that I got to wondering what they're like on dead men. So I looked. It was like a fat white earthworm.

Dark-haired, lively, gay, tender.

—What about you? Have you already done it?

She flushes.

—Me, I've never done it, not so far.

Holding my hand tightly.

—I wouldn't mind doing it with you.

In my arms.

—It scares me.

Her tensed little body.

—I've heard that it hurts, is that true?

Her arms round my waist.

—I promised myself that I'd only do it with somebody I love.

She remains silent a long moment.

—Now, of course, it's as you like.

Seized by a brief shivering.

—Tomorrow, I'll be able to say that I've made love.

A jerky laugh.

—Tomorrow, I'll be a woman.

A womanizer, her husband has betrayed her again and again, each time she blames herself for it, but she's jealous, she knows she shouldn't let him see it but it's beyond her power, it always happens the same way, he has some extra work to do at the office, or friends he has to go and see, or a business dinner, he comes home late at night, doesn't say a word, sometimes his shirt collar has lipstick on it or there are a few woman's hairs on his jacket, he gets into bed without touching her, as though contact with her was distasteful to him, he falls asleep, and the next morning it's the same until the day comes when he doesn't even bother to lie, he doesn't return home for a week or two, however much time it takes him to come to his senses, for it is a form of madness, then, afterward, he goes back to doing exactly the same thing, twice she followed him and saw him with women who were neither charming, nor beautiful, nor even well dressed, nothing, one of them was so fat that she was spilling out of the awful coat she had on, that's what he was sleeping with, whereas she is still very youthful, really ten times younger than these overweight whores, she believes she knows where he picks them up, it's in the bar that's just across from his office, there's always a clump of them in there waiting for nothing but that, one day, during a period when everything was going all right, she had tried to speak seriously with him, tried to find out what wasn't working with her, he looked at her a long time right in the eye and then smiled a humiliating smile that she will never forget, she was able to tell, she could feel deep down he considered her a pitiful helpless creature, she could have killed him, she asked him what she had to do to attain the performances of the pigs he was screwing, he just shrugged his shoulders and left, she thought she'd never see him again, but no there he was the same evening, calm as could be and with some flowers for her, as if a bouquet could make her forget a humiliation as awful as this, indeed since then she doesn't know who she is, what kind of woman she is, how she is to proceed, how she is to live, she would like to go to bed with another man so that she can find out from him whether she's normal or not, she had heard that there are women that do things in bed that make men go crazy, what can those things be?

The off-white stockings over the very firm thighs.

I'm wearing colored lace.

Seated on the wall, her legs dangling. She is frail, with light blond hair.

—Do you know any dirty words?

Her eyes of stinging blue.

—Not words like *shit,* everybody knows those.

She lowers her head toward her breast as though she could become invisible that way.

—Words like the ones my big sister uses when she goes with boys. I follow them without her knowing.

A shiver narrows her shoulders.

—At night in my bed, I repeat them, only some of them I haven't heard properly, I can't get too close because if they saw me my sister would beat me up.

She jumps down onto the grass.

—If you like I'll tell you all the dirty words I know, but first you must catch me and pull off my underpants.

On the table, the tips of her fingers caressing the roots of mine to the point of irritation.

—I'm good at caresses, aren't I?

Her hand slid flat underneath my hand.

—I'm perverse.

Such a young face and yet so grave.

—Sometimes I ask myself, am I a believer or am I not?

She smooths down her hair with the flat of her hand.

—For me to be on the side of God, sex has to be on the side of God.

Her long hair encowls her round white shoulders.

—If what I've done with men is a sin, then I'm headed for hell.

Thinking a moment.

—Hell doesn't frighten me. I'm a daughter of fire.

I wish your eyes were things that were touching my skin.

—You've never seen my room? One day you must come home with me. There's no risk, my parents work all day. We could fuck in my own little bed.

Her smile is sharp.

—I've never been jumped in that bed.

Her fingers alight very delicately on the tip of my sex, which she pinches between her thumb and index through my trousers.

—You have a hard-on.

She tries to sit on my lap.

—No, not here.

—Here or elsewhere, I don't care. There's a cock and I want it.

That night, in the hotel corridor adorned with antique furniture, having left the room in her knickers and her breasts bare, she runs to a window from which for a few seconds she admires the illuminated city, then turns around and comes back very slowly, simulating a manner of impressive dignity, she is sputtering with laughter, making fun of herself, she passes a finger over her lips, spies the servants' stairs in a corner, starts up, halts on one of the steps, thighs wide apart, so that in the transparent white knickers she is wearing can been seen the shadow of her sex, which she caresses with a slithering hand, her tongue protruding, making her hair fly about her shoulders with a movement of her head, suddenly alerted by a sound she races back to the room where she hides herself as in a shelter, posed on the bed with arms reaching out to embrace.

—Come quick, hold me tight, I want to be a whore.

Her head comes up to my shoulder, she has shiny black hair, thick lips with greasy makeup, her nipples point behind a thin blouse, her short red skirt clings to her hips.

—I'm not from round here. Are you?

She is staring at her own reflection in the window of a department store before which we are standing.

—A little while ago there was a man who told me I looked like a whore. Do you think so?

With a finger she pushes a strand of hair out of the way behind her ear.

—In the street I don't want to have the look of a whore.

Coming closer.

—I want to have the look of a young girl.

Her arm under my jacket.

—What do you like best? A whore or a young girl?

Hanging on to my belt.

—My parents don't know anything, otherwise, you know, my father would kill me!

Holding me tight against her.

—It's not in order to give you an erection, I'm sure you've got one already, I have that effect on every man, but the truth is that for me it all started the day I saw my father naked with his thing standing up. I was only eight, but I remember as though it were yesterday. I'll remember it all my life, that great big stiff thing of his. I think it got something going in me. As soon as I could I wanted to see other ones. It affects me the same way each time, my heart starts beating faster, it's like my pussy was moving, I don't know how to describe it, I have my mouth full of saliva just because I'm imagining your cock getting big. I know a place at the back of an entranceway where there's a nook, it's pretty big, that's where I do it, you avoid the price of a room and you're just as well off. It's not far, come.

—He was lying on the bed fully dressed. Without any warning, I grabbed him by the hair and shoved his head in between my thighs.

An icy glance.

—He hadn't the the foggiest idea what to do, the ass-hole! Me, I like to be sucked good and deep inside, so that I can really feel the tongue.

Now facing out the window.

—I collected my panties, my handbag, and I left him there. I slammed the door. I felt like my cunt was diseased. I took a taxi to get home faster and got under a shower.

Golden mass of her blond hair.

—In any case, as soon as I've fucked I have this need to wash all over, to purify myself.

You have to walk on tiptoe down the long hall running the length of that comfortable apartment.

She is in the lead, a finger to her lips. We are a little fearful but even more excited by what she's promised we would see.

At the very end the door opens onto her parents' bedroom. A big bed with a pink bedspread, several chests of drawers, a sofa, some other smaller pieces of furniture, a mirror, lamps on the tables, two armchairs, pink too, and finally a wardrobe, waxed, gleaming, its hinges polished.

Mysteriously, she opens one door, then another. The shelves are filled from top to bottom. On the shelf within our reach are piles of her mother's knickers and brassieres, to be unfolded one by one and touched and sniffed on condition that we not rumple them.

When we shall have left the room and the apartment after having paid the tithe levied upon our curiousity, hers will be the task of refolding all that lingerie as it had been before.

She writes:

I'm mad with desire to make love with you. Just writing that I become tense. I would truly like to be a woman with you. I think of nothing else all day long.

Being in a train with you after a night of lovemaking. Escalating desire and its fulfillment. I dream of it. I'm obsessed by you, by all the pathos of sex, by its violence.

Behind the window of the train just about to leave, she sucks her finger and signals to him to do the same. "That's how we can make love together all the time, anywhere we like."

She knew how to wait for him in some public place,

dancing with herself, wearing a crooked little smile, strong in her lack of constraint.

She could stop before a store window and give it a sudden long lick with her tongue before skipping merrily away.

—All the stupidities you hear uttered about that, it's unbelievable!

Unlovely, in a suit of conventional cut.

—I've been searching for love for twenty years. Twenty years of looking for the man who is capable of loving me, capable of giving me an orgasm. I'm still looking. And there are thousands of others like me, it's the truth.

The salon is a vast white room containng heavy low sofas.

The couples are dispersed in a semi-darkness. A young woman in a green satin evening dress that exposes her entirely naked back is stunningly beautiful.

Smiles are exchanged.

—I brought you here. Don't touch any of these whores. You're with me, you stay with me. If you want something, I have my own room just upstairs. Excite yourself over them as much as you like, but your juice is for me.

Curled up tight, she's asleep, her hair covering part of

her face, her neck, and shoulders. It's the hour at which we separate after a night spent together.

A finger on her breast. She growls. Sitting on the edge of the bed, I call her in a low voice, I know she can hear me.

Her eyes shut, as though in pain:

—I want to suck you again.

Be hard. Cracking with desire. Balls up under the belly. Head of your cock ready to explode.

Day and night. Night and day. Stay like that, you excite me.

My mouth, it's my sex.

Look at my mouth, it's eating you.

I could speak for hours, as though the lips of my sex were making love to you. With my tongue I suck away on the head of your cock.

I could suck you for hours.

Be big, big, big and hard for me.

In the packed crowd in the bus, her hand which, despite my whispered protestations, slips in through the opened fly and begins its sharp quick caresses.

—I want you to discharge before the next stop.

I danced with him only once, at his village fête, they were peasants, I was on vacation, at the start I danced normally, but when I realized I was getting all of them excited I began to rub on them, I could tell it was driving the tall one out of his mind, he was shoving his cock into my belly as though he were screwing me, after three of four dances together he was sure he was going to get in, I went back to my hotel like a good girl, he didn't dare to follow me, the next day I left the place, one evening I was at home all by myself, I don't know what led me to think about this guy, it seemed like I had his cock up against me, I took the first train and arrived at his house in the middle of the night, he couldn't believe it, he was only wearing trousers, I pushed him into the house, I shut the door and sucked him off at the entrance to the kitchen, there was a smell of soup and the dog didn't stop barking while I was sucking him, he yelled at the dog to shut up, I visualized the scene, me sucking off this big asshole who had, by the way, a tiny little cock, I would've liked to be able to see myself, I said to myself, "Aren't you a little off your rocker my poor girl? Jumping onto a train to come and suck this wee bit of a cock when you've got thousands just asking for it two steps from your front door?" So I told him to finish the job himself, that I was going to watch him do it, he had hands that were so big his little cock about disappeared inside them, you could hardly see the tip while he was at work, an idea suddenly came into my head, I told him I wanted to go abroad with him, that I'd wait for him the next day at the hotel with the plane tickets, next day I had the tickets, can you see me in the plane with that bumpkin? I set off all alone, it's strange, it's at that moment that I began to see life differently.

The red perfume of her soul.

Did you know that when you come in my mouth you have the face of Christ?

She lives with her mother in a two-room apartment on the top floor of a dilapidated building, so I found out when I went over to her table because she was sitting on her chair in such a way that you made out a beginning of white skin above the darker edge of her stocking, and because that position was inviting and she knew it.

We shortly arrived at what was on my mind, which she was ready enough to fall in with, the only difficulty, if it represented one, was that she preferred us to go to her apartment rather than to some hotel.

On the stairs, lit only by the daylight entering through some sort of glazed loopholes, she several times trails her hand over my sex, each time emitting a little exclamation ending with a sucking sound.

—You're already in great form!

She opens the door to an antiquated living room lit by an overhead fixture decorated with pendants and minus a few bulbs removed out of economy, with a vinegary odor pervading the whole place.

—This is mother.

Sunk down upon a deformed sofa there indeed sits a lady of a certain age who gleefully extends her fingertips for me to kiss.

—You step up close to her, she sucks you. After that I take care of you in the next room. I do it for her, she can't go out anymore.

The old lady, reaching a hand behind my knee, pulls me to her and, the opening obtained, thrusts her head through it, her tongue out, little gurgles of satisfaction coming from her throat.

—Do what you have to do, I'm not watching.

Curled up in a gray armchair with worn-out springs, the girl is leafing through a book.

—I can tell you, though, that each time it does do something to me. You'll see in a minute.

I start by licking right at the top of the ear, then work downward along the edge, then I come back up again, I do that several times, wetting it well with my saliva, and at the end I stick my tongue suddenly into the hole. It's as though I were being buggered.

The middle of the night, in the hotel room near the station, lit by the ruddy glow of lights coming from the street.

—I don't know if I loved him.

Hesitation.

—At the beginning, yes, maybe. We were both so young. Also we both had the same ambitions, that counts.

Flattened, her breasts shine in a sliver of light from outside.

—Unfortunately, in bed it was zero. He couldn't control himself, we were no sooner lying down than it was already over with.

A touching youthfulness.

—And then he annoyed me with his worrying about getting me pregnant. His everlasting contraceptives, it used to turn me off entirely, made me feel sick, I can't stand those things in my mouth.

Sudden entry of sadness into her gaze.

—Now my life has changed. I fuck as I like, I don't care a damn about the rest.

—Do you ever see him?

She laughs inwardly, her mordant, troubled eyes remaining fixed on me.

—From time to time. It amuses me to give him another try.

—I knew I'd become an old woman the day I noticed men were finding excuses for not staying alone with me, for not accompanying me when I went out, for not being seen in my presence. However, I could have made them acquainted with something they won't find anywhere else: pleasure begot of despair.

Her hand grabbing the sex inside the trousers.

—Oh! What is this I feel here! . . .

—How do you want me? In black stockings? In white

stockings? With or without a brassiere? I'll come the way you want me.

The smile of the department store salesgirl, agreeably perfumed.

If that were possible, I'd halt men in the street and ask them to show me their cocks.

For you, I can be everything you want.

—Lie down there on the bed, don't move, wait, I'll be back.

She goes into the bathroom and locks herself in. I can hear the little sounds caused by her picking things up and putting them down on the surface around the washbasin. I stub out a cigarette in the ashtray on the bedside table.

I think I have heard a clock somewhere strike two or three in the morning. In the street the honking of a car.

The bathroom door opens. She has put on a sort of mauve net dress through which you see, silhouetted against the light behind her, the separation of her thighs and a few hairs of her sex. She is very made up. Her breasts appear as round shadows.

—I'm your whore. I still have the taste of semen in my mouth. All those rotten bastards I sucked during the day, but I'm always ready for your cock. It's you who taught me that whores reserve their best juice for their pimp. First I'm putting out the lights, then I steal toward you, you won't even hear me, I'll take it in my mouth without you realizing I'm there. My tongue is special, it's a viper's tongue.

—I don't mind, but then we don't make love, I'll just do something silly, but not anything else.

She comes into the bedroom wearing only her thick, high-rising knickers picturing Mickey Mouse dancing a jig, and into which is set, directly in front of her sex, a lace panel.

Women's lingerie strewn about the floor near the bed. A blue shoe lies tipped on its side.

I can no longer order chocolate mousse in a restaurant since knowing that at your house I ate some mixed with your fuck.

In a few minutes my train will be due.

She pulls from her pocket a series of small sheets of paper.

—It's that girl I told you about who's written to me. When she came to sleep at my place I took such good care of her that I think she's a little bit in love with me. I'm keeping her in sight. After a few years of cock, I'll have her.

—Sometimes when I have to wait before crossing the street I stare at a man I choose at random among those on the sidewalk opposite. I keep my eyes fastened on him until we have the green light and we cross. That's when I position myself so that I rub up against him and I show the tip of my tongue. That drives them crazy. They get this insane light in their eyes. As for me, it's like when you have a nerve exposed.

The big stockroom at the textiles warehouse is full of various kinds of merchandise, there are stacks of new mattresses.

The person in charge is a woman of about thirty, very made up, as dressed up as her means permit.

I am still only a child about to enter adolescence, and yet, inexplicably, I have sensed a kind of unidentifiable disorder which emanates from that woman when you find yourself alone with her. One of her thumbnails has a very spatulate shape, a detail rendering her rather mysterious to me.

—Get a mattress down.

—That's not what we were told to do, is it?

—I give the orders here. Get a mattress down from that pile and put it on the floor.

Perched at the top of the stepladder, I manage to slide

a mattress down onto the wooden floor, she helps me lay it flat and at once falls on it on her back.

—Have you already seen a woman on a bed?

I don't understand exactly what she's referring to.

With a quick gesture she uncovers her thighs all the way to the slight mound her sex makes inside her panties.

—Come over here.

She takes my hand, pulls it, pulls me over.

—You mean to say you're still a virgin? I'll show you what to do, it's not difficult.

She undresses me haphazardly, gets out her breasts, fits my mouth up against them, telling me to suck, which I do mechanically while she fondles me.

—I hope you've got a big one. It's a big weewee I'm after.

Then she starts teaching me how to make love. The discovery of this pleasure with an experienced woman seems to infuse powers in me that until then I had never known.

—Every Saturday morning you'll be on duty in the stockroom. We'll both be on duty.

She gets herself back together.

—What a lot of fuck you have in you, you little pig, you've spattered it all over my thighs.

Will you explain to me what the words mean, to fuck to death?

—Put the tip of your pecker into the little jam pot, I'll

suck it for you. That's what I like for breakfast. I suck and then eat a bit of toast. Eventually, you'll see the knob's all sticky with jam, crumbs, and some come that seeps out in spite of you. Then I pump, lick everything. You wind up with a pecker that's nice and clean.

Sitting on the rumpled bed in the early morning, half-dressed, her legs bent underneath her and her thighs spread wide, her pink sex draws air into itself by a rapid series of gulping contractions.

—Fill it up again. See, it's still hungry. Look what it is able to do.

This part of her body has become the seat of odd self-induced twitchings.

—I have something all the way at the back of my pussy that others don't have. Something that makes cocks go crazy.

Haloed by glowing youthfulness, her face, to which sweat has stuck a few locks of hair, is diabolically beautiful.

For you I shall be wife, mistress, mother.

She puts her arms lovingly round me as we dawdle along the sunny streets.

A burst of laughter.

—Why are you laughing?

She coyly lifts one shoulder and gives a girlish toss of her head.

—Because, before coming to get you, I told him to do the dishes, to scrub the floor with a brush, and I know he's doing it now.

Her light step.

—I dreamt of you all night long. We were in a house in the country, a pretty white house, but all filled up inside with trash, and you were telling me that was where you were going to have me. I had some kind of liqueur flowing within my body.

—Take me. Sock it to me. Bang it in there as many times as you can, let me feel it all the way to the bottom. Push. Shove. Go on, harder. Wreck my pussy. And hold on to your juice, hold on to it! Keep going. Some more. Dig. Stuff it all in. Wait for my juice before you come. I want us to come together. I'll do the rest to you afterward. You can fuck me in the mouth. I can handle cocks down my throat. Brush. Brush. Scrape. Bite my breasts. If you want I'll turn over right now. I'm as big behind as in front. Put your finger in there. Stick it in, stick it up me, so that I can feel it in my belly. Talk to me. Say filthy things to me. Tell me I'm a fucking cock-in-the-ass whore, that I've already drained a hundred cocks inside me. Talk to me close to my ear. Spit inside it. I like to be covered with slobber. It's like watery fuck. Don't let go, you bastard, keep in there, I'm going to come!

—I'm getting married, but it's as if I were going to the slaughterhouse.

On a stone bench in a shaded corner of a public garden extending along the river whose murmurings I can hear.

—I'm wet. Touch.

She takes my hand, draws it under her skirt in between her thighs.

—Feel it?

If you could have seen the face on this guy when he began to feel me up and he realized that my undies were all silk, it scared the shit out of him, I saw then that he wasn't going to jump me.

I would like to dirty my soul.

She sinks down out of sight, stretching herself full length upon the banquette. Impatient fingers search for the zipper.

The mouth is large, hot, laden with saliva, the tongue, pointed, now probes, enwraps, thrills, now with all its wetted surface broadens the caress. Slippery little animal, she is once again seated on the banquette beside me.

—Why didn't you want to come?

Hanging on to my arm, her head almost lying in her mass of hair deployed on the table.

—I want your juice.

She grips my wrist so tightly it hurts.

—Don't you know that I want juice?

Humble.

—I would have dried you off with my hair.

—I know you, oh yes.

—No.

—I tell you I know you.

—No.

—I never forget the face of a customer.

—I'm not a customer.

—Don't say you've never come upstairs with me!

—Never.

—Liar. You men, you're all rotten liars. In any case if you wanted to today, I'd say no.

—I don't want to.

—You're not going to try and make me believe you don't like prostitutes? All men like prostitutes. I know what I'm talking about.

—I didn't say I didn't like prostitutes.

—So? What do you want?

—Nothing. I'm looking at you.

—And how do you think I look?

—Good.

—Good for a fuck?

—Good for a fuck.

—Then we're going upstairs?

—No.

—Faggot. Go get stuffed.

Beckoning with her hand from the car parked amongst others side by side along the street.

The window is rolled down.

—I'm not expensive, and for the price you get a little girl who takes her clothes off and who's good at sucking it.

Her broad smile brings the flat of her tongue into sight.

—And then I do whatever you want.

Wicked dark eyes.

She writes:

It's one o'clock in the morning. I've just had a cigarette. I smoked it with all my desire. Tonight, I'm crazy for you.

My mouth which keeps opening.

My black undies.

I would like to be hideously sluttish. I haven't been enough of a slut with you.

I like it when you have your brute look. Men look at you then. I'm sure they're afraid of you. Before, you used to scare me too. You would scare me but I liked it. When you tighten your lips and make your eyes like slits your jaw becomes square. You look like a killer then. Could you kill someone? Answer me. I want to know. I often think about it: could you kill someone? You won't reply? You are capable of killing someone. That's why you turn me on.

—My mother is nothing at all, hardly a woman, her life consists of her children and cooking for my father, that failure, he's always talking about other women or telling disgusting stories, but apart from my mother and maybe a fast go with another woman, he's never fucked anybody, I'd swear to it, he's just waiting for one thing, to know that I'm doing it, but with him I act like a good little girl, it'd give that jerk too much pleasure to fuck by procuration, since my childhood all I've heard is mostly stuff coming from him about women, talking in front of my brother, my mother, and me about all the ones he'd had, in his imagination, doesn't take long to figure that out, and my mother who would listen to it all without saying anything always busy cooking the little dishes for him that he liked best so as to keep the asshole happy dreaming up hot lays in his head, I bet if I brought home three big strong guys, because his ideal man is a big muscular stud, one who might slap him once or twice in the chops without his even lifting a finger, I bet if I told him I was being jumped by all three at the same time he'd be proud of me, that half-wit, he's afraid of growing old, of dying, that's all he thinks about, his death, he used to dish that out to us at table morning, noon, and night when I lived at home, he's a wreck, gone, I don't know how my mother could've gone to bed with him and let herself have kids with him on top of it all.

In the grand hall of the hotel.
—Am I not the prettiest of them all?

A certain audaciousness, a kind of wild elegance, an unerring sense of how to dress, she is indeed the most attractive woman there.

—And I know also that I'm the best fucker too.

In the elevator.

—You and I, we'd only live in grand hotels. As for the bill, no question of any such thing, I'm here. I've never yet taken money for it, but I wouldn't hesitate. You'd like that? In bed with a good fucker and, when called upon, a good earner too.

—You're lying.

—There is no life without lies.

—You lie with everything. With words. With your smiles. Your glances. With your body.

—The only truth is death, and death I'll keep away from.

—I want life. So I lie.

—How do you handle all these men?

—I manage.

—I know what you think of men.

—I don't think anything. They fuck me when I want them to, that's all.

—If that's all, then what are you lying for? Why are you always in the act of lying?

—You want to know? Because they all expect a girl like me to lie to them.

—You have the blood of a slut in your veins.

—What are you blaming in me? My strength?

—Have you ever said anything true to a man?

—To a man? I tell him to fuck me, or I tell him I'm going to fuck him, that and nothing else.

Emerging suddenly out of the darkness, she hands me her bag to free her hands.

—You're going to see.

She grasps the hem of her tight wool skirt and jerks it up, revealing her loose black knickers.

—Did you see?

She slowly turns all the way around.

—And now what are you going to do?

Her skirt back in place, her dark eyes riveted upon mine, with one hand she mimics the masturbating of a man's sex.

—Piece of shit.

Holding it between her puckered lips she smokes the cigarette that she has fitted between my big toe and the one next to it.

—It's as good as sucking you off. See how my mouth is swollen? What I would like to see at the same time as I smoke is your cock. Open your fly and let it out.

The room is enveloped in smoke.

She loves her daughter, but she's incapable of giving her any tenderness, something she can't explain stops her from even touching her, from entertaining a physical relation with her, her mother behaved with her in the same way, she was cherished, well fed, well dressed, but tenderness was nonexistent, there was never any proof of love, she suffered from that, becoming introverted very early, undeniably it has had an effect on her married life, she's been divorced twice, that's what she would like to preserve her daughter from, because she sees to it that she wants for nothing despite the fact that it hasn't always been easy financially, but with this adolescent she lacks the courage to go further, there's a kind of wall between them, it's probably as disagreeable for the one as for the other just as it must have been for her own mother, but one cannot fly in the face of these psychological barriers, unconsciously she is jealous of her daughter's success, sometimes she wants to reduce her to nothing, deep down in herself she's the first to suffer for it, but in daily life it's impossible for her to behave differently, she knows in advance that she will be jealous of her daughter's joy if ever she finds a man to make her happy, nothing links them deeply, she can neither kiss her nor grant her moments of tenderness as one usually does with children, it's as though she were her mother through an error.

A little round nose on the serious face looking down.

—There is nothing more beautiful than a sex in erection.

She wants to know just where I am at home, if I am going to masturbate while listening to her talk to me on the telephone.

—At the end, let your juice spurt out onto the floor. I'll imagine it on the carpet, a little white gelatinous puddle. Do it slowly, I'll tell you when you have to come.

Dawn, underneath the dulled makeup, her hollowed features, weariness in the depths of her eyes, an abandon, a sad lassitude.

—You love who did you say?
—Cocks.

—I don't dare talk to you about your sweet smell that casts a spell over me.

Laughing out loud, she throws herself heavily onto the bed, her arms outflung, her eyes shut.

—You know what he does to me, that maniac?

She rubs her freshly made-up lips one against the other.

—He reads girlie magazines in front of me, then he goes off and gets into bed and falls right to sleep. He doesn't even fool with himself, the eunuch.

She hooks her brassiere.

—Some day I shall have to bring him some semen so that he finds out at last what it is!

—I want to suck you right down to the marrow. First I want you to have a lot of juice so that it will flow for a long time into my mouth. I'll suck you, you'll melt little by little, until there'll be nothing left of you except your cock. Then I'll suck it some more and it'll shrink until there'll be nothing left of you at all.

—Are you tired?
—No.
On her knees on the bed.
—Let's play the flower game.
A childish face.
—You ask me what flower I prefer and I'll reply.
Hands clasped in front of her mouth.
—You start.
—What flower do you like best?
—The penis. But the big variety.
Lifting her head up straight.
—Ask me some more.
—What other flower do you like?
—The pussy. But very open.
She bites her lips the while laughing.
—There's one more left.
—Which?
—The little hole in the behind. But licked nice and clean.

—From age nine to fifteen, I prepared myself for the act of giving myself to a one and only man.

—I'm a frigid whore.

—At my death I want all the men who have fucked me to be gathered round my bed. I'm sure Death will be impressed and will spare me.

—Frig is all I do, but I have a girlfriend who pumps.

Young breasts glimpsed through the plunging neckline of her white bodice.

—Do you know what I do when I'm good and hot? I fetch them out and without ceasing to stroke them I bring them up between my breasts so that they discharge there. I don't wash for several days after. It sticks, it dries on my skin, it has an odor I can smell when I'm walking in the street just by bending my head a little. I bet you don't know the smell of semen as well as I do.

—He's sick with jealousy, he doesn't love her, she never loved him, she doesn't even remember the reason she married him, to have someone near, so as not to drift forever from one to the other, he is without intelligence, without concern for intelligence, he can hardly handle his work, she said nothing for two years, did everyting to be an irreproachable wife, one day she couldn't put up with it any longer, he was treating her worse than he treated his dog, so she decided to go out every night, at first the disputes had been violent, he even struck her, but she held on, he never had the means to offer her those things a woman needs, now she buys herself what she wants, she has her little tricks, her little arrangements, the men she goes out with are generous, they give her orgasms, which he never succeeded in doing, she has to have that, she's a real woman, she doesn't come home until daybreak, he's still awake waiting for her, every time its the same question, where has she been? first she tried lying to him, but what was the point? She ended up by telling him the truth, he looked completely bewildered, stunned, he stared at her like an idiot, sitting on the radiator in the bedroom, he started to cry, he asked her to forgive him, she went and shut herself into the shower, he got into a rage, he was pounding on the door with his fists, she got scared and opened the door, he'd cut his face with a knife, he was covered in blood, a horrible sight, before calling the doctor she cleaned him up with washcloths, he surrendered to her like a child, at one moment he murmured mommy, she slapped him, he sank down on the tiled floor sobbing, she washed her hands and left him where he was, she got dressed, jumped into a taxi, had the driver take her to someone's place, and made love with that someone all day long.

Insects from different families passing each other on a blade of grass. A little touching of antennae, then each goes his own way.

—I sit in the public gardens, I have nothing on underneath, I show them my tuft.

—She would come into our room every evening to kiss us. In the beginning she never touched me, maybe because I was the eldest. It was my brother who slept beside me that told me. I called him a liar. But one night, inside my pajamas I too felt her hand, which she would slip under the covers to jerk us off, because she frigged the two of us at the same time. Finally my brother would let out little whimpering sounds, little sighs. Me, it made me bite my teeth together. That went on for a long time, until one night she just woke me up. In the darkness I couldn't see her, I couldn't even see her form. The sheet was lifted, she got it out as usual, then she bent down. The next morning, in the kitchen, while she was preparing our breakfast, I would watch her attending to this and that as though it weren't she that did it. She would seem to me so beyond reproach that I would wonder if I hadn't dreamt it.

She does all sorts of things to keep me there, even wrapping her arms around me and kissing me, she being still a young woman, but with a sallow complexion and missing teeth, dark gaps revealed by the would-be sensual smile.

—You don't think kissing is part of fucking?

In the morning as I leave home, I know I'm going to go there. It turns me upside down. Some days, while I'm getting ready, I say to myself that I won't go, that I musn't go, but I know in advance that nothing will be able to stop me.

In front of the café, instead of entering I walk round the block two or three times to put off the moment when it'll begin. I walk down the street as though in a hurry, I can hear the sound of my heels on the sidewalk, I think of the prostitutes who walk to and fro.

When I can stand it no longer, I go in and sit down at a table, the employees know me, the waiters shake hands with me.

As soon as a man looks at me with any amount of insistence I go down to the toilets. He soon arrives. I latch the door shut, I lift my skirt, I put one foot on the toilet bowl and get myself stuffed.

Sometimes, in the café, I go directly up to the table where the man is sitting. I look him straight in the eye and say: "I'm going downstairs to the toilets. You going to come?" It gets me wildly excited. There are days when, as soon as the door's shut, I tell them I want to suck them off, even if it's not true.

If they don't come inside me, I finish them off by hand or with a sucking, but most of the time it's not necessary, they get going in there at top speed. Some days, when the idea appeals to me, I tell them I'm a prostitute.

The white fluffiness of her blouse, open and revealing her brassiere. Her disarrayed hair on the hollowed pillow.

The room dims little by little as evening draws on. We enter into a warm silence. Perhaps, outside, the world has stopped existing.

—What are you doing?

—Looking at you.

—How do I look?

—Pretty.

—Pretty and what else?

—Pretty and exciting.

—Look.

For panties she has on little more than a ribbon.

—Say something to me.

—What?

—Tell me what it means to sharpen a pencil.

—Wait for me, I've a rendezvous, but I'll be finished at midnight. Even before. It's my guy who masturbates in front of me, you remember him?

Just to see you ejaculate without touching you, your sex enormous, afterward I'll lick you clean with gratitude, delight, and respect.

From up at the open window looking down upon the street.

—All those cocks passing by, cocks I shall never know.

—I jerked them, that was the first thing I did, then one day there was a fellow who put his cock in my mouth and told me to suck it, I didn't know how, I was afraid of looking like an idiot, when the fuck flowed into my mouth I reacted with loathing, I spat it all out, I wasn't yet fourteen but from that day on I did it without being asked, what I didn't want was penetration, I wanted to stay a virgin for the one I would love, stupid fool that I was, I would've done better to do it right off, especially since at my age men are really hot for it, to fuck a young girl there isn't anything they weren't ready to do, I placed great hopes on penetration, but the first time it was a fiasco, as it usually is, I should have known it, the day after losing my cherry I had two men in the afternoon, one on a banquette in a bar, I got it all over his pants.

—You can do whatever you want with me, but I don't want anybody touching my breasts.

She writes:
Sunday
I made love with you at the end of the afternoon, in early evening.
I made love with you so much that I ordered you to fondle yourself through your trousers during the meeting you were

attending, to draw down your jacket so that no one could see you had an erection. I gave you pleasure with your cock only part of the way in me, I did it for a long time. Never before had I done it as much with you at a distance.

You had your sex in me and I made love to you. I was very happy to feel you inside my sex.

I've found a divine pair of shoes in black satin.

Sitting opposite her in the bar that has the big upholstered leather armchairs.

She sucks the straw in her drink with which she stirs the ice cubes in her glass, which, according to her, are little testicles.

At a gesture of my hand she opens her thighs a little, enabling me to make out, in the shadowy hollow, the line of her panties.

—Don't do anything, just lie back and take what comes and discharge, as long as you're feeling good.

After a nervous dance, standing on the bed, she falls to her knees, buries my head underneath her, and before I can succeed in getting hold of her, is down on all fours on the floor, her undone dress revealing fine black lingerie.

—I'm so beautiful in summer.

The morning is clear, its light a tender blue.
She walks slowly down the broad sanded paths of the garden. Clustered rhododendrons are blooming on the islands of fresh grass.

—Tell me a lie.
—I love you.
—Bastard.

In an unattractive, cramped little room, its rather tall window curtainless, her bed is just a wide mattress lying on the floor.

She writes:
We'll be a pair of sharp-clawed tigers.

—When I'm wearing a light dress with a very short skirt I am easily taken for a schoolgirl, they walk alongside of me saying whatever enters their heads, talking very fast, they want to know if I've already seen a man's sex, if I've touched any, how many, if I know what it is to frig, if I know what it is to suck off, how about making love, don't I want to, they have big cars, beautiful apartments, no one's there, they're very nice, I shouldn't be afraid, they give presents, once I went with one of them, he had a studio with works of art and the bed was round, he disappeared and then came back in a dressing gown, I could see it bulging where it came together in front, he poured us drinks, I told him I didn't drink alcohol, he found me some horrible green mint tasting stuff, books were piled on a little table, he opened one and sat down beside me on the arm of the chair, the erotic illustrations were old-fashioned, he caressed the back of my neck, he had on some perfume that made me giddy, he took my hand and placed it inside his gown, his thing was thick but short, from there on there was no more fancy talk, it was nothing but a cock to unload and a cunt to ream, it was clear that he was sure that with me it was a done deal, so I started to cry, to make a lot of noise, coming out with heartrending sobs, my little one, he said to me, what's the matter my little one? the seasoned seducer of little girls, that's how he came on, I told him I was a penniless country girl, needed help to pay for a hotel, he gave me some money and an address nearby, and promised to join me there, that same night, on the doorstep he looked so embarassed that I burst out laughing and said to him, and I quote, Monsieur you have been so kind, could I ask you one last favor, I would like to have a look at your cock, I thought he was going to slap me but he slammed the door in my face, in the street I went on laughing about it all by myself.

Screened from the lights, the public bench is further

protected by the vegetation in the gardens where the fair is taking place.

—I don't mind letting you touch, but afterward you won't want to take me out anymore.

Popular music in the distance.

—Touch a bit but just a little.

Coarse hairs.

—I have my own room not far away, but tonight I can't. Because the day after tomorrow I shall have my period, and I have noticed that if a man gets on top of me it comes earlier and lasts longer.

Entwined shadows.

—What I can do is give you a blow job, meanwhile you've got to be on the lookout, if ever we were seen it'd be bad for me. It happened to a girlfriend of mine.

From her bag she takes out an obscene utensil.

—What do you think of it?

In a flash it has disappeared underneath her skirt. Caressing herself with its tip:

—No man has one as long as this.

Placing it in my hands.

—Suck it. I've already had others suck it. Get it good and wet and then I'll put it in. I brought it to use in front of you. It's a beautiful tool, don't you think?

Between her lips.

—Now, there's a mouthful. I had another one. A few days ago I was by myself, I sucked it a while, I was reading. Finally it got my tongue so hot I wanted to bite into it. I took a piece out of it. Do you know what it was? A carrot. I ate it all.

—As soon as the clock strikes five in the afternoon I have this terrible urge to make love.

—My husband didn't even want to hear about it. He doesn't care either way, whether I keep it or get rid of it.

At night, one's alone. One cannot sleep.

—I've thought of it for hours and hours. I didn't believe it could happen to me.

He was asleep his hands clenched.

—Is that a crime or is it not?

He was snoring.

—A life is a life, but with the first three I had my hands full.

She went alone to the hospital. She passed a man whose face was covered with blood. She gasped, she was seized by fear. She should have had someone come with her.

The doctor had the look of a torturer. He talked on and on about the forthcoming procedure. Run away? But that would have had to have been possible. Now it was too late. They practically accuse you of murder, at least they imply it, showing their disgust for you.

There's the metallic clatter of surgical instruments. The assistant may provide some moral support. She has pinched lips. You are unable to catch her eye. You would think it is some chore she's performing against her will, disapprovingly. You touch the depths of humiliation. You fear that things are not going as they should.

The doctor shows you the embryo he has just extracted. A vague gray shape that looks sort of like a mushroom. You walk out of there alone.

—I'm on the street, looking for a pass. You find me cute, you stop. Would pay me a lot?

In front of me she rubs her body up and down on the iron post between her thighs, scratching it voluptuously with her nails.

I love the summer for its sexual moistness.

She writes:
I would like the night to get under both our skins simultaneously.

I am so beautiful tonight, dressed all in pink, stretched out on the floor where together we could spend such terrific moments.

—The condensed milk that comes in a tube, squeeze some out onto the tip and I'll lick it off, as if you had come.

Sweetly pleading:

—Make love to my little feet.

—His older sister has big heavy tits inside black brassieres, at night in the room they share she manicures her toenails, her legs bent to bring her feet up close, her skirt pulled up to her panties which are often black too, his big sister caresses her tits while looking at them in the mirror, her big thing is full of hairs, he sees it nearly every night when she gets undressed, in bed there are times when she moans and the bed shakes, one day his big sister came up close to him and stuck her hand in his underpants, he was scared, he didn't understand what she was after, his big sister shuts herself in the outside toilet with boys who come out of there all red, not long ago he heard his big sister say when I get fuck I'm happy, so happy, she also said I could eat fuck every day, what is it about this fuck that it's so good, one of these days he'd surely find out, it must be another of those disgusting female things, because his big sister she's a slut, even his father says so, he told their mother your daughter has all the makings of a whore, that day when he was so mad at her he even yelled all you're fit for is buggery, *buggery,* there was another word he didn't know, in their bedroom like before, one night when he was sleepy and his big sister wouldn't turn out the light because she was ironing her clothes on the little table, he didn't mind coming right out and telling her you're a fuck-in-the-ass, that made her laugh, she stuck out her tongue, she wetted the end of her finger and fooled with herself down underneath there, he didn't understand that either, what he would like would be for his big sister to tell him everything that girls do, but he's afraid to ask, it must be really disgusting, or else, because he thought of something else, or else he could very quietly go and sneak into his big sister's bed some night when she is moaning and the bed's shaking, he'd be stark naked, no pajamas, he'd find out what she'd do after that, on the washing day they hang the laundry to dry at the window, there are always one or two pairs of his big sister's black underwear, he has his homework to do but he can't help looking up at them, he imagines them when his big sister has them on when she spreads her legs and pulls her feet up close to polish her toenails, and you can see between her thighs.

I have become nothing but longing itself. I await you.

In front of her breakfast, seated in an armchair that is too deep for her, her face still smudged by the sleepless night, her breasts bare beneath my jacket hanging over her shoulders.

—If I were really powerful, I would have a huge castle with slaves who would bring me my breakfast every morning and when they came near I would frig them a little to get them all hard. Then they'd line up in a row in front of me and I'd eat my buttered rolls while looking at them.

On the little square, deserted and poorly lit, in front of a wall her silhouetted figure wrapped in a big baggy dark duffel coat that she holds closed with both hands.

—With me you know what you're buying, I always display the merchandise before accepting payment.

She opens her coat to reveal heavy breasts, a swollen stomach, broad hips in a pair of soiled knickers and thighs that are too fat squeezed into stockings held up by straining garters.

—For kinky stuff I offer bargain prices.

She covers up. The wind is cold.

She writes:

ORGASM. *Having you lying fragile in my arms. Making love to you from top to bottom. I possess you by way of my hands.*

—I'm jumping up and down on a cock!

Her legs bent at the knee, sitting on her calves, she jumps rhythmically up and down on the bed.

—I'm sucking a cock!

She bends forward, advancing her lips.

—I'm coming all over a cock!

Thighs spread, her hair in disarray, her head jerking convulsively, a prolonged cry that thins as it comes to an end.

She lies back with her head reposing upon her folded arms. In a tone of comic disappointment:

—Cock's all gone.

The brass buckle of a belt.

This afternoon, waiting for you, I turned myself into something marvelous in red and black, all silk.

—One day I'll show you all the places where I've had myself a fucking in the street.

Tall in her expensive dresses, she is never back before the wee hours, often half-drunk, whether accompanied home by someone else or after having wandered the streets for a long time, making lengthy stops at the counters of the cafés where her state and her old-fashioned elegance draw about her a crowd of men, most of them workers having a last cup of coffee before going on to their jobs.

—If one of them attracts my notice, I become so obscene with him that nothing can stop him from following me.

Dead-tired, she literally crumples upon the mauve leather sofa.

—I expect nothing from them. It's just their desire that interests me. These poor jerks think that just having a cock and two balls between their legs makes them irresistible. They know nothing about love, about women, nothing about the subtleties of perversion.

She yawns, her head thrown back.

—I insist that if they want to jump me they take me near the place where they work. Not one out of three dares to. They don't want to be seen with a high-class whore like me, in an evening dress or furs.

A disdainful laugh.

—You know, there was one who didn't know that dresses slit to the waist exist, it drove him out of his mind seeing me walking alongside him, my thighs showing at every step. That's all he could look at, fascinated as if by a snake. At a certain moment I touched him, just to check it out. No erection at all. It was too much for him, he looked as though he thought he was in another world.

Stretching out her legs, she kicks off her shoes onto the carpet in front of her.

—One day I ended up by finding one. A mountain of muscle with an idiot look. That one there, whatever I wanted he wanted too. He took me to the construction site where he was working. They were putting up a big building. I followed him, we went up on a creaking elevator and at what floor we got off I don't know, all over the place were old sacks, plaster, planks, cement. It galvanized me. It was I that undressed him. I sank back onto a pile of rubble and opened up, holding out my arms to him. These oversized guys are worse than animals. He had come even before he had crouched down in front of me. I felt like cleaning his cock but he smelled too strongly of sweat.

Slouching further down onto the sofa.

—That was yesterday, yesterday morning, or the day before, I don't remember. It seems to me that nowadays they no longer know how to arouse a woman. You, for example, what would you do to excite me right here, right now?

A rush of tears.

—And first of all, why don't you want to fuck me anymore? We did use to make love together once upon a time, didn't we?

She hammers her heels angrily upon the floor.

—Why don't you want me anymore? You don't love me. You've never loved me.

She bends all the way forward, as though her body had snapped in two at the waist. She is reduced to a shape made up of cloth and hair and racked by sobs.

Suddenly sitting up, her cheeks streaked with mascara.

—It's because I'm not enough of a whore? Then teach me to be. Once you've got me thoroughly trained, do you think maybe you'll love me?

Her long slender hand with its reddish brown nails lies over her sex.

—Masturbating over my panties, is that all right?

The sun is a downy milkiness behind the violet-colored drapes over the windows.

She enters the shop where, so as to have my opinion, she has me look at various models of clothing, some of which earn my approval, others my disdain.

With the help of the salesgirl she carries those I approve of to the cubicle, asking me to come along and then sending away the assistant after she has placed everything on a clothes tree and on a stool.

She has me come into the cubicle and shuts the curtain behind us, sweeps the stool clear, steps out of her panties which she hangs on the clothes tree above the clothing already there, she pulls up her narrow leather skirt, sits down on the stool, and leans back with her legs stretched wide apart.

—Lift me up and stick it to me. I'll hang there impaled on your cock.

Late at night, leaning back against the cloth-covered wall of the hotel room, slim in her velvet skirt, wearing a little colored ribbon around her neck, her gaze liquid, she bites into a green apple.

—Take me in yours arms and kill me.

She has been sitting alone for a long while at the café table, crossing and uncrossing her legs, which gleam inside tinted stockings.

I leave the café, smiling in her direction. She follows me.

In the room.

—Go ahead, but I'll be very cold.

—It's not my mother, that dumb cow, but my father and my brother who told me I would surely be getting them soon. Two men. I made myself sick just thinking about it. It came in the middle of the night. It was the warmth of the blood that woke me. I switched on the light. I lifted the sheet and saw blood on my thighs. I crammed a handkerchief inside. The next morning, there was still more of it. I didn't dare say anything to my mother and the other two made my flesh crawl. I went to a friend's house. She didn't have hers yet but her mother was very kind, she gave me all I needed. The whole thing left me with a feeling of anxiety. Every time it starts, the first day I feel ill at ease, frightened.

—She is bent over, sloshing buckets of water on the stone stairs, the bottom of her gray dress is tucked up, showing the wide strip of white cloth of her petticoat and sometimes, when she bends over even further, the top of her thighs show in stockings that nothing seems to be holding up, there's a wind blowing, it's cold in his shorts with his bare thighs and knees, he feels queasy, it's early in the morning, he drank a whole bowl of tepid milky coffee with bits of bread soaking in it, maybe he wants to throw up, the rinsing water is clean, but dirty the water the woman is using to plunge the floor cloth into, it smells sour, musty, rotten, rancid, mildewed, the house itself has the same sour, musty, rotten, rancid, mildewed odor, all the houses in the street have the same odor, all the women in these houses have the same odor, dirty water courses down their legs, their stockings are wet with dirty water, their legs, their thighs are dirty, why shouldn't their eyes and their mouths be dirty too, and what do they do these women when they're not dumping buckets of water on the stone stairs, they go out to meet the men who come back dirty from their work, the skin of their faces dirty, their hands dirty, their clothes dirty, their shoes dirty, they have dirty laughs when they take the women in their arms, when they hold them tight against them and kiss them, two dirty mouths glued to each other, when it's time to go home to the house there's always dirt somewhere in the kitchen, on the gas ring, in a plate forgotten in the sink, a glass half full of wine, the crumbs of lunch still on the oil-cloth, a basin no one has put away, the big woman whose legs were soaked by the dirty water prepares dinner for the man and the child in silence, the water has dried on her stockings, but the dirt hasn't disappeared, the stockings are full of it, the air is full of it, the light from the big yellow bulb is full of it, the old brown scaly walls in whose corners dirty little insects are nesting, on the window the night sticks like glue, the man goes to bed, the woman follows him, you can hear them kissing again, making dirty noises, laughing and gargling in the bed with its dirty sheets, also one knows confusedly that it is from this dirt that one was born and will one day die, that tomorrow there will still be a dirty floorcloth in the thick water which will splash onto the stockings of the woman bent over the stone stairs, that it will be windy, that it will be cold.

Hallway carpeting worn through in places.

—Are you married?

—Maybe.

—I ask you that because I don't understand why a married man would visit a prostitute.

The door of the room is open.

—You can't see a thing in these lousy rooms of theirs.

Dull, syrupy light from the bulb inside its cardboard shade.

—There. We're going to have some fun, the two of us. Going to let me have my little gift?

Coming closer.

—Hey, look at that. That's a real hard-on! Like me to frig it a little there inside your pants? I enjoy the feel of something hard in a pair of pants.

Her hand surrounds the sex.

—At home the lady of the house doesn't do that to you, does she?

She writes:
I'm your little whore.
childlike
perverse
female
foul-minded
girlish
authoritarian
sensitive
whorish

tender
dissolute
ignorant
naive and whorish

Sumputous in a short light brown dress, her thighs half-exposed, quick agile legs turning into mobile feet in delightful matching shoes on the car pedals.

—Have you seen the traffic we've got tonight?

It is indeed so thick that you can only advance at a crawl.

—Imagine now that I stop in the middle of the avenue and suck you off. Especially you who take a while to come. What would happen?

Her hands on the wheel, her tongue out.

—As soon as I think of sucking, I get pins and needles at the tip of my tongue.

The girls outside the doors to the hotels.

—Which one would you go for?

None of them has anything seductive about her.

—I love to come to this street. It's not so much because of the whores. Of course that does do a little something to me, but what really gives me a rise is the men who stand there staring at them for hours without being able to go up with one for lack of money. Imagine all those desires, all those men with stiff cocks, it makes me shiver, makes my teeth clench. I would like to go and suck them all off, right there, standing in the street, for free. When I come by here, I feel sex all over my body, I am unable to think of anything else.

Getup deriving from a sailor suit, pleated blue skirt, sleeveless white middy blouse affording glimpses of underarm areas, a little beret perched on the back of her head.

—Outside, at night, I find a spot between two cars, I sit down and all he needs to do is let me have it, but I'm always the one that puts it in me.

She holds an imaginary member in her hand, brings it slowly toward her, spreads her legs, directs it to her sex, her hips dancing.

—I look around to see if anyone's coming, I keep watch.

Rubbing herself upon the introduced member.

—As soon as I see someone, I stop everything, I put my arms around him, as if we were lovers, except that my pussy is still full and I continue feeling it. The people go away, we start in again.

Her belly undulates.

—I always tell them to hurry up and come, that gets them in there tight and it's fun for me.

She backs off.

—I squeeze them so hard that they generally aren't able to hold out long.

A delicate face.

—Between cars, cock-sucking isn't practical.

She whirls round. Her white panties momentarily visible beneath her outspread skirt.

—Sometimes, I stay on afterward and start in again on the first one that comes by. Once I did ten in a row. It was like a dream. I couldn't believe it was me. I don't know why, but I thought about my parents.

Sitting on the bed.

—One night, do you know what I imagined? That I'd just finished up with one, that my father came by, that he didn't recognize me, and that I took him too without him realizing anything.

She settles herself in the bed, fluffs up the pillow beneath her head.

—Can you picture it? My father's cock, me stuffing it into myself. If I could do it in these conditions, I think I'd have a real orgasm, not like with the others. With them I don't do anything. It's they that come. I don't care. What I like is picking them up, pulling their cocks out and putting them inside me. There are some who want us to get together again. They really don't understand anything, the poor cunts. I want cock. I don't want chitchat. I do that at least once a week, for example, on my way home from work. It's evening, you can hardly see their faces. I start thinking about it, I can't prevent myself. I sit down between two cars. What would be good would be to be able to do it during daytime too.

She stretches.

—Do you like me as a little sailor? Undress me, it's hot, I want to be naked in this heat. I like you to undress me because you do it slowly and you begin with the shoes. Once anyone touches my shoes my nerves contract. I think I would have liked it if that had been the way it happened to me the first time. It was a skinny little guy. I was wearing a pair of panties that I hated, my mother had insisted on buying them for me, I was holding back my tears, I was very miserable. Also, I was afraid that he wouldn't find my pussy big enough. It's true that it is small, I was ashamed of it. I'd heard that women who have made love a lot have very big pussies, I was very anxious, the room was gloomy, wallpaper with eagles on it, some flying around and others perched on the branches of bare trees. At that time in my life I only thought about kissing, about making love with someone you love.

She writes:

Be a cock erected for me. I'll make you come with my tears which little by little will bring you to a climax.

And my hair in disarray glides over your lips, your sex, with an immense sweetness.

Her lips are two swollen lumps of pale, damp flesh.

—The way I am right now, I could handle the fuck in every man alive, have it all over me, dripping from my mouth onto my neck and breasts. Come and rip open my dress, I want to become a fire of burning woman. I no longer have the strength to move. My whole body is hard. Come and set me free. I'm the first woman in the world. I'm Eve. I am going to vie with God. I know I am a match for Him. I'm being fucked by all the men who have ever put it into me. I have all their members inside me at the same time. I'm rigid with cock. Tear off my dress, otherwise I'll go mad.